When the
Wicked Rest

a collection of
509 Crime Stories

by Colin Conway

When the Wicked Rest

Copyright © 2024 Colin Conway

All rights reserved. No portion of this book may be reproduced or used in any form without the prior written permission of the copyright owner(s), except for the use of brief quotations in a book review.

Cover Design by Rob Williams

ISBN: 978-1-961030-17-6

Original Ink Press, an imprint of High Speed Creative, LLC
1521 N. Argonne Road, #C-205
Spokane Valley, WA 99212

This is a work of fiction. While real locations add authenticity to the story, all characters appearing in this book are fictitious. Any resemblance to actual persons, living or dead, is purely coincidental.

Visit the author's website at colinconway.com

Table of Contents

What is the 509?

Separated by the Cascade Range, Washington State is divided into two distinctly different climates and cultures.

The western side of the Cascades is home to Seattle, its 34 inches of annual rainfall, and the incredibly weird and smelly Gum Wall. Most of the state's wealth and political power are concentrated in and around this enormous city. The residents of this area know the prosperity that has come from being the home of Microsoft, Amazon, Boeing, and Starbucks.

To the east of the Cascade Mountains lies nearly two-thirds of the entire state, a lot of which is used for agriculture. Washington State leads the nation in producing apples, it is the second-largest potato grower, and it's the fourth for providing wheat.

This eastern part of the state can enjoy more than 170 days of sunshine each year, which is important when there are more than 200 lakes nearby. However, the beautiful summers are offset by harsh winters, with average snowfall reaching 47 inches and the average high hovering around 37°.

While five telephone area codes provide service to the westside, only 509 covers everything east of the Cascades, a staggering twenty-one counties.

Of these, Spokane County is the largest with an estimated population of 506,000.

Foreword

There's an adage that says there's no rest for the wicked. The etymology of this statement is found in the Bible. Isaiah 57:21 reads, "There is no peace," says my God, "for the wicked." When I thought about the third collection of the 509 Crime Short Stories, I immediately considered this assertion. I thought it had a cool ring and would be evocative of the stories within.

It didn't hurt that the adage was also the title of a 1988 album from Ozzy Osbourne. The record came out while I was in the Army, and it's one of my personal favorites. The moment I heard the first single, "Miracle Man," I had to purchase the cassette so I could listen to it in my car and on my Walkman.

The release was heavier than Ozzy's earlier work because of Zakk Wylde, his new guitarist. Each song was crunchy and unlike anything I'd heard before. I repeatedly listened to that album from the first song until the last. This was during the halcyon days of hair metal, so there was a lot of competition for my listening pleasure.

I loved every song on *No Rest for the Wicked*, not just the radio releases. There was another single off that album, "Crazy Babies." It also was great, but my favorite song might be "Bloodbath in Paradise" with its references to Charles Manson and the Manson Family murders.

While some hair bands were singing how "Every Rose Has Its Thorn" and others were crooning about girls who were barely "Seventeen," Ozzy touched on some seriously dark subjects. There were no party songs on *No*

Rest for the Wicked—the Godfather of Heavy Metal didn't do that type of thing.

There were no ballads either, even though conventional wisdom at the time said rock bands had to have one because they attracted female listeners. The slowest song on *No Rest for the Wicked* was "Fire in the Sky" and it was still heavy as hell.

Ozzy came to rock our faces off and he delivered.

***

There was something special about music before it could be streamed. We listened to our albums and cassettes all the way through without skipping songs. When compact discs came along, it made bouncing from song to song easier. Often, though, I still listened to every tune on my albums. It seemed the right thing to do.

Streaming services discourage newer generations from discovering all the songs on an album. They want listeners to experience the most popular music in a chosen genre with the help of algorithms. Streaming services don't care about quality; they only care that the listener stay engaged.

It's unlikely any streaming service will offer "Hero" over "Miracle Man." The latter was a popular song because of its radio release and subsequent rotation on MTV. The former was a hidden song on the cassette and CD releases of *No Rest for the Wicked*. It's an excellent song but only the true Ozzy fans heard it.

Musicians create their songs and structure their records in a certain way. Sometimes I love the way an album comes together. Each song raises the stakes and takes the listener (me) to a new plateau. There are even slow albums that do that. I might be a metal guy, but

Sade's *Diamond Life* (1984) burned so hot it almost tore a hole in my heart. To this day, I'll listen to the album in its entirety.

At the other end of the spectrum were albums that seem tossed together without consideration for the listener. Nothing was worse than the energy created by a truly great song being wasted when it was followed by a wimpy ballad. If you've read my stuff for any length of time, you know I love Mötley Crüe. The worst track listing decision the boys ever made was following up the rollicking "Kickstart My Heart" with the gutless "Without You" on *Dr. Feelgood* (1989). I've probably mashed the next button on that song more than any other in my life. I'd blame their drug usage, but the Crüe was sober for that album.

But the girls liked that song and I guess that's what mattered.

***

A couple of years ago, I had the wild idea of creating an anthology series. I would invite some crime fiction friends to play in the 509 and let them run amok. We built each collection around a central theme. The first concerned the wholesale eviction of a low-rent apartment community. The second dealt with a missing bag of hamburgers. The third centered on the impending death of a legendary driver.

The collections were a blast to put together. Working with other authors was a fun experience, since writing is often a lonely endeavor. Unfortunately, the 509 Crime Anthologies were not great sellers.

I should have predicted that from my purchasing behaviors. I love Lawrence Block's books. I also adore his short stories and have bought several of his collections. Yet I'm lukewarm to anthologies he's been included in. Eh, I think, what else of Larry's can I read?

To continue with the musical theme above, I wouldn't consider buying a *Now That's What I Call Rock* compilation CD because it had an Ozzy song included. Even if that album was the only place I could get that specific song, I would hold out for the tune to appear on a greatest hits collection. I'm imagining many of my faithful 509 readers did just that with my 509 Crime Anthologies.

The short stories I wrote for those collections mattered to the tapestry of the main 509 series, yet they lingered in a self-imposed obscurity. I couldn't insist my readers buy something they didn't want. Not even Lee Child or Stephen King could insist their fans do so.

I had assembled two other short story collections—*Murder by Any Other Name* and *Black and Blue in the Lilac City*. They included numerous tales that affected the full-length novels.

The solution to my anthology problem was to create a third 509 short story collection. This would allow those readers who didn't want to purchase a *Now That's What I Call Crime Fiction* anthology to catch up on what had occurred. I would also include some other stories to round out the new compilation and hope I could make most of my readers happy.

It's like a greatest hits album. You might have heard some songs before, but there are others you likely haven't.

***

This is where I twisted the previously mentioned

adage and allowed the wicked to rest.

Putting together a short story collection is significantly less work than writing a new novel. The individual tales were already composed, so it was essentially an act of remixing. Some updated editing occurred on all the stories. One tale had a significant rewrite. Overall, it was a nice run through some tales I hadn't touched in a while.

If you're a fan of the streaming services, jump about this compilation in any order you like. It's your book now. Do with it as you wish but know this—there are no ballads in this collection.

On the other hand, if you're like me and a fan of tradition, I hope you'll read them in order. I assembled the stories this way for a reason. Each should exhilarate you and push you toward the next. When you're finished, catch your breath, and get ready for the next 509 book.

There are many more tales on the way.

The wicked aren't resting any more.

Colin Conway
Spring 2024

When the
Wicked Rest

Hope Evicted

"What're those?" Dorothy Givens asked.

Fred Tresko leaned forward and dropped a hand onto a stack of yellow documents sitting at the corner of his desk. "You know what these are."

She scooted to the edge of her chair so she could read the header on the top paper. "Thirty-day notices?"

"Don't act surprised. We gotta do this to make sure no Gonzaga snotnose can buy one of those tenants another month. If that happens and the snow falls, we're screwed. We'll have to wait until spring."

Dorothy slid the top document out from under Fred's hand. As she read, she muttered, "I never thought."

Fred fell back into his swivel chair. It groaned and squeaked under his weight. "Are you kidding?"

She glanced up.

He asked, "What did you think we've been doing these past two years?" The question was filled with derisive nonbelief.

Embarrassed, Dorothy turned away and pretended to examine Fred's industry awards on the wall.

"Well?"

She continued to stare at the framed certificates. "You know how things are. I just thought maybe it might not happen. That maybe there might be a reprieve or something."

The swivel chair moaned as Fred leaned forward again. "You mean you want the Hope to stay the way it is?"

She might have answered honestly if that question

didn't contain more of his derision. Dorothy looked down at the final eviction notice. The legal words blurred together.

Fred Tresko folded his arms and leaned on the edge of his desk. "Because of the housing shortage, the market is hot."

Not looking directly at him, she said, "I know."

"For nearly a decade."

"I know that, too, Fred."

Dorothy hated when he spoke to her in this manner. He ran Sterling Management and was her employer. She'd learned plenty from the man in their years together, but there were times when Fred Tresko lectured people as if they were obstinate children and he was a teacher in a one-room schoolhouse.

"Demand for housing is at an all-time high," Fred continued. "Marry that with the city council's delusions to implement socialistic rent controls, and what've you got?"

She knew, but no matter what word she selected, Fred would pick another just to show he was smarter. Therefore, she remained quiet and simply shrugged.

"Urgency." He slapped his hands together, and Dorothy looked up. It was an involuntary reaction, and she regretted it immediately. Fred's eyes narrowed now that they'd contacted hers. "Goddamned urgency is what we've got. How did you not know that?"

Another shrug.

"That's why we've had to work so closely with those commie bastards. Give them all sorts of concessions and do an ass-kissing dance any time one of them calls. I'll tell you what." He pointed at her. "Whenever one of them found a camera, they'd wring their hands about what we were doing," Fred wrung his hands and made a sorrowful face.

Dorothy looked down again. Maintaining eye contact with Fred only encouraged him to rant. She needed to let it peter out, or she'd be there for an hour.

"But, oh boy, get them behind doors, and it was a different story. They loved how this project would clean up that cesspool. They loved what it would mean to the neighborhood and the city's coffers. Duplicitous bastards."

His voice had softened, and the engine for the anti-council express seemed to be losing steam. Had she continued to feign interest in his tirade, he would have moved onto some other soapbox—perhaps the tax implications of the whole thing. She hated when he talked about taxes.

Fred harrumphed. "Why this town wants to be like Seattle is beyond me. Give these people the power to vote, and what do they do? They vote morons into positions of authority." He grunted as if to signal the end of his diatribe.

She noticed the ticking of the clock on the wall. Fred began tapping in rhythm with the second hand. Dorothy looked up to find him studying her.

"Now," Fred said, "it's time for us to do our jobs and get that building cleaned out."

"Where are those people going to live?"

Fred shifted his weight, and his chair creaked its displeasure. "Not our problem."

"But that's a hundred and three apartments."

"Only seventy-two. The rest were smart enough to leave when we warned them."

"Well—"

"Our job isn't to play social worker, Dorothy—"

"I know—"

"Our job is to help the property owner make money."

"But—"

"But what?" Fred snapped.

Dorothy stiffened. She didn't know how to respond. She turned away from Fred's reddening face.

"Well?"

She offered, "This seems sudden," and regretted the words as soon as they passed her lips.

"Are you serious? This is in no way sudden. It's thirty-one days until Halloween, and we announced this event more than two years ago. Everybody's been on month-to-month leases for that whole time."

Dorothy's shoulders slumped. She did not look forward to delivering any of these notices.

"Twenty-four months," Fred said and tapped his desk harder. "Twenty-four months we've talked about this, yet seventy-two residents hung around until we have to push them out."

"A number of them were foreign families desperate for a place to live."

"They could have gone elsewhere."

"But the housing shortage. You said."

Fred waved her off. "We posted notices in the lobby. From day one. Over seven hundred days ago. And any time one of them got ripped down, you replaced them. Am I right?"

Dorothy reluctantly nodded. She or one of her staff had repeatedly replaced the ripped-down notices over the last two years.

"And still seventy-two stubborn and, might I add, foolish people decided to make us evict them. They caused this situation. Not us. This is their fault. Well, I'll tell you what. If they want us to be the bad guy, that's fine by me. We can do that."

Dorothy didn't want to be the bad guy. "I never really believed it would come to this."

Fred clucked his tongue. "Don't be naïve. Certified letters went out Friday, so the tenants should be getting them today. If they check their mail. That's why you," he pointed at her, "need to post these," he stabbed the stack of yellow notices with the same finger, "on every door."

"Yeah."

"There are enough in here for the vacant units, too. I don't want some mealy-mouthed lawyer saying we didn't give proper notice to every damn tenant."

"Even Lester?"

Lester was the owner of the Lamplighter, the bar on the lower level of the Hope.

"Oh, no," Fred said. "I'll deliver Lester's personally. That sumbitch is going to be a pleasure to evict." He tapped the stack of notices again. "There're extras to put on the restroom doors, too. Don't chintz out with where you hang them. Above and beyond. Got it?"

Dorothy nodded.

"Any questions?"

She felt silly asking it, but she did anyway. "Are they tearing it down?"

"Tearing it down?"

Lowering her head, she almost whispered. "For the new hotel."

"The fuck?"

"Never mind."

"Tear it down? No one is tearing anything down."

She kept her head lowered but lifted her eyes to him—the way a beat dog begs the forgiveness of its owner. "But some in the building have said—"

"You're listening to junkies and life's other losers? How would they have any idea what's going on? No wonder you thought this day would never come." Fred rolled his eyes. "Jesus, Dorothy, think, will you? Why would anyone tear it down? Construction costs are out the ass. No, they're going to gut the Hope to its bones and then start from the inside out."

"That's what I thought." She had thought that, but so many in the building seemed certain it was getting torn down that she had begun to question what she knew.

Fred continued. "Two years ago, Mrs. Caldwell signed a master lease for the building with a developer out of Portland. I already told you this."

She nodded. He had explained it before, but she dealt daily with short-term apartment leases, not commercial contracts.

"It's a forty-year deal," Fred continued, "with a slew of options on the backend. Good for her, good for her estate, and good for the developer. But she can't turn it over until the building gets an enema. Understand?"

Dorothy winced, but she got his meaning. Her eyes hovered on the notice she still held. She had yet to put it back on the stack.

"You got another question," he said. "I can see it. Go ahead and ask. I don't want you wandering around in that building listening to those ding-dongs."

This question didn't feel silly, but still she whispered. "What about me?"

"Huh?"

Dorothy straightened, pulled her shoulders back, and repeated, "What about me?"

Fred crossed his arms over his belly. "What about you?"

"I have an apartment there. And my job."

"You'll be fine."

"What about Anita and Earl?"

"Don't worry about Anita and Earl. They're not your concern."

She looked away. Dorothy cared deeply for Anita and didn't know what the woman planned to do after this. Earl was a cantankerous man who made caring for him hard. She worried about him, but in a Christian way, not the friendship manner she had with Anita.

"You," Fred said, "you're the onsite manager, so you'll be taken care of. Trust me. The developer's gonna need your help, too."

Dorothy cocked her head. "How do you know?"

"What do you mean, how do I know? I know. I've been around these things before. They'll need your help finding where things are. Helping the subs learn their way around. Direct them to turn-offs and electrical panels. Whatever they need."

"That sounds like a better job for Earl, him being the maintenance man and all."

Fred's face pinched. "Earl Ricci is not a people person. Quite frankly, I'm glad we don't have to work with him anymore. After the contractor gets set up and firing on all cylinders, I'll find something permanent for you."

"Do you promise?"

"Oh, yeah." Fred Tresko closed his eyes and nodded. "Definitely. For sure. You're my girl."

***

Dorothy left the Paulsen Center's sixth floor where the Sterling Management offices were located and walked the ten blocks to the Hope Apartments.

It was cool out, but she barely noticed. Her mind was occupied with the conversation she'd just had with Fred.

The notices in her hands felt like a bag of bricks—a bag of heavy, smoldering bricks.

At the apartment's entrance, Vernon Brown crouched near the door. When she neared, Vernon blew out a long stream of blue smoke and flicked his cigarette into the street.

"Sorry, Miss Dorothy."

She stopped and considered him. Vernon was in his late-sixties, and his once ebony skin was now an ashy gray. He wore a tattered sweatshirt, khaki pants, and blue running shoes. His yellowed teeth were visible behind a forced smile.

"For what?" Dorothy asked.

"Smokin' in the doorway. I know the rules."

Vernon had lived in the building for more than a decade. Currently unemployed, he filled his recent days by hanging outside the east entrance of the building. Throughout the years, Dorothy had helped the man find temporary work or necessary social services.

Her eyes drifted to the yellow notices in her hands.

"I won't do it again," he said and pulled open the door for Dorothy.

"It no longer matters," she muttered.

Vernon's smile faded as she passed by.

***

Dorothy sat in her office and stared at the stack of notices. She had set them on a chair along the far wall. A knock on the door refocused her attention.

"Yes?"

The door opened, and Earl Ricci stepped in. He was a short, pale man with a protruding beer belly. Underneath a canvas Carhartt jacket, he wore a dark brown T-shirt and dirty blue jeans. "Why's the door closed?"

"I wanted some time to myself."

Earl watched her for a second before saying, "I can go."

She shook her head. "What do you need?"

"Nothing. That Vietnamese family on three keeps jamming crap down the sink then complainin' for me to fix it."

Dorothy sighed.

"It's not racial," Earl said defensively. "I'm just tired of them doing it, is all. They're fine people even if their food does smell kinda gross."

She lowered her gaze.

"What's wrong, Dottie?"

"They're evicting us."

"Yeah. Okay. That ain't exactly news, now is it?"

"It's finally official." She pointed to the stack of papers in the corner.

He grabbed the top sheet and read it. "What's this happy horseshit?"

"*Earl.*"

"Uh-huh," he said absently as his eyes scanned the page.

"Don't uh-huh me. We still have an example to set."

Earl waved the yellow paper now. "We're officially on the clock is what this is saying. Thirty days. Has anyone talked to us about jobs afterward? No. Not a peep. You think maybe they already got something lined up for us elsewhere?"

"Don't be naïve," she muttered. Fred's voice echoed in her ears.

"What's that mean?"

She explained to Earl her meeting at the offices of Sterling Management and the lie told there.

"Fred lied?" Earl asked. "Are you sure?"

"As sure as this building is getting evicted."

Earl stared at the yellow notice he held. "But how could you tell?"

She bent over and put her head in her hands. "I just could."

***

Earl took the notices to post so Dorothy could remain in her office. She accomplished little more than moving papers from one pile to another as she waited for the inevitable first person to arrive and complain.

About forty minutes after Earl left, Alma Moore shuffled into the manager's office. Her hands gripped an aluminum walker that rattled and clanged with every step. Alma's gray wig was canted slightly on her head, and her thick glasses were dirty. A crinkled notice stuck out of the pocket of her muumuu.

"Doomsday is upon us." Her voice shook as she spoke. Alma pulled the notice from her pocket. "I got another one in the mail, too. Said exactly the same."

"I'm sorry."

"Why? You didn't do this."

"Still."

Alma dropped the paper into the wastebasket. "I don't know why they gotta tell me twice. I got the message months ago."

"It's the law, Ms. Moore. It requires both delivery methods. Just to make sure."

The older woman made a dismissive snort before pulling a wrinkled envelope from her pocket.

"What's this?" Dorothy asked.

"Rent," Alma said. "It's the first, ain't it?"

Dorothy opened the envelope. Inside was a money order with no entry made on the payee line. Every month, she received many checks like this and often filled them in for the tenants.

"I thought about not paying," Alma said, "but it didn't seem right. God wouldn't approve."

Dorothy stared at the empty payee line on the money order and fingered the silver cross around her neck. "I doubt everyone will be as understanding as you."

"They won't be," Alma said. "I'm sure of that."

***

Anita Moss, the assistant manager, bounded into the office around ten, an hour before her shift started. She had an eviction notice in hand. "You forget to tell me something?"

Dorothy looked up. "Just got them this morning."

"I stayed up late last night reading a book. Thought I would sleep in this morning. Didn't figure anything this exciting would happen today."

"I didn't know it was going to happen, either."

"Earl woke me up as he was taping notices to all the doors. That is not a quiet man."

"I am sorry, Anita. I should have come told you right away."

Anita dropped into the chair in front of the desk and reread the yellow notice. "We knew it was gonna happen. Hell, it makes sense it would be today being the first and all. Am I gonna find one in my mailbox, too?"

"Yeah."

"Figures."

Dorothy watched her assistant and a woman she thought of as a friend. "I'm embarrassed to say, I thought they might not go through with it."

Anita's brow furrowed. "How so?"

"State agencies are always showing up at the last moment. I thought something like that might happen with us." Dorothy felt like crying.

Anita leaned forward. "Hey, now. You can't be this way around the residents. They can't see you sad. You need to be strong. We all gotta be strong."

Dorothy nodded.

"Pull yourself together, Mother Hen. Do what you do. Make sure everyone is okay."

A sad smile creased Dorothy's face.

"Because I sure as hell can't pull that off." Anita crumbled her notice into a ball and tossed it into the wastebasket. "No one would believe me." She headed for the door. "I might be a little late today."

Dorothy eyed her. Anita appeared ready for work. In fact, Dorothy had been about to ask if she wanted to start early. "Where are you headed?"

"The Lamplighter."

"For?"

"What do you think?"

Dorothy stared at her. "You can't drink before work."

"What is Fred going to do? Fire me? That would be putting me out of my misery. If you want, you should join me."

Dorothy considered grabbing a drink. She didn't usually, but— Her face tightened.

"What?" Anita asked.

"Lester."

Anita rolled her eyes. "He's going to be butt hurt over this."

"Especially since Fred's delivering his notice personally."

"He's not."

Dorothy nodded. "He seemed to take great delight in the idea."

"The ass."

"You go ahead and have a drink with the man. Sweet talk him a little. He fancies you."

"And tell him what exactly?"

"That residents need him to hang around for the month."

"He doesn't want to close, Dorothy. I think he had the expectation he would be allowed to stay."

She sighed. "Sweet talk him, okay? I'll be over in a bit to break the bad news and let him yell at me."

***

Shortly before noon, Dorothy walked out of the Hope's main entrance and rounded the corner of Main Street to the front of the building where the Lamplighter was located. She could have entered through the building's lobby—the backway into the Lamplighter, but she avoided that way as much as possible. That entry felt seedy while the front door felt official. It was the little things that Dorothy held onto now.

Lester Poole had purchased the bar almost twenty-five years ago and made no modifications to the business. The heyday for the Lamplighter had been during the Nixon administration. That's also when it had its last remodel. Low yellow tables with short-backed, black vinyl chairs were scattered about. The gold shag carpet was worn to the concrete in places of high foot traffic.

The jukebox contained only music from the seventies, and the bar still smelled of stale cigarette smoke, although smoking inside an establishment had been outlawed for more than twenty years.

Anita sat at the bar and sipped a clear-colored drink while Lester cooed to her. He was tall and thin, and he wore a pale blue button-up and dark slacks. His eyes drifted to Dorothy after she entered. His smile melted, and he straightened.

"The devil," Lester said.

"Mind your manners," Anita snapped. "She ain't the devil."

"Then she's his agent."

Anita lifted her drink. "Then so am I. You gonna be rude to me, too?"

Lester's smile returned. "No, Nita, never. Not you."

"Then treat Dottie like you would me."

The bartender's gaze drifted back to Dorothy. "You here to deliver more bad news."

She noticed the two yellow eviction notices on his bar. "Seems you've gotten enough for one day."

"Tresko made a special trip down to see little ol' me." Lester reached over and crumbled one of the notices. "All this time, that motherfucker—"

"Lester," Anita whispered.

"—said I'd have a chance to negotiate a new lease whenever the developers took over. I bet they're gonna bring in one of those fancy beer joints—a gastropub." Lester air-quoted the last word. "Hipsters and their fucking craft beers."

"*Lester*," Anita said.

"It's okay," Dorothy said. "He's got every right to be mad. Lester, I've never handled your lease. I only do the apartments."

He sneered. "Well, anytime I talked with the man, he shined me on with some bullshit about how I was his guy, and he was going to take care of me."

Those words sounded familiar to Dorothy.

"Guess I'm out on the street now."

"Everyone else is losing their homes," Dorothy said.

"Yeah? Well, I'm losing my business."

Anita shook her empty drink, which caused the ice cubes to clink together. "Dottie and me are losing our jobs *and* our homes, so we win." She cast a sideways glance to Dorothy. "That doesn't sound like a win, though, does it?"

Lester took the tumbler from Anita. "That true, Dottie? You both out of jobs and on the street?"

"That's right."

The bartender grabbed a bottle of Seagram's and filled Anita's glass. He then put a splash of tonic on top and dropped a fresh lime in. "There you go, doll."

Anita took the drink and sipped deeply.

"Maybe you should ease up," Dorothy said.

The assistant manager pulled the glass from her lips. "What're they gonna do?" she muttered.

From the back bar, Lester shook a cigarette free from a pack of Camels. He stuck it in his mouth and lifted a lighter.

Dottie frowned. "You can't smoke in here."

Several patrons turned to look at them.

With the Camel tucked tightly between his lips, Lester motioned toward Anita. "Like the woman said, what're they gonna do?"

"There are rules to be followed."

"Says who?" Lester asked. He then ignited his lighter and inhaled deeply.

"The law."

"Let 'em write me a ticket." Smoke billowed from the bartender's mouth as he spoke. "What's the worst that's gonna happen? They shut down my bar? I'll be kicked out before it works its way through the system."

Dorothy looked around, helpless. "You need to pay your rent."

Lester inhaled from his cigarette again. This time he held the smoke for a while, then exhaled from the corner of his mouth. "I ain't paying shit."

"But you have to."

"Make me."

Dorothy glanced at Anita then back to Lester. "You have a lease."

"Which Tresko refused to extend. Let him hire an attorney to kick me out for non-payment. I'll get out under the wire. Until then, I'm staying rent-free. Makin' bank for an emergency nest egg."

Dorothy stared at Lester. "They won't allow it."

"We'll see about that."

Anita's eyelids drooped slightly, and she remained silent.

"If I can give you some advice," Lester said. He pointed the two fingers that held his cigarette. "Get while the getting's good. They're only using you while you serve a purpose." Lester sucked on the cigarette before continuing. "When you no longer serve a purpose, well, that's when they kick you to the curb."

Anita thunked her glass on the bar two times. "Amen."

"The only person you should have loyalty to," Lester continued, "is you." He looked to Anita. "Both of you. Look out for number one as they say."

"We need to go," Dorothy said, reaching for her assistant manager.

Anita pulled her arm away. "I'm taking a sick day."

"A sick day? You never call in sick."

She slowly nodded her head. "I'm not feelin' so well."

"You were fine an hour ago."

"Well, now I'm not. What are they gonna do?"

Lester chuckled. "Yeah. What are they gonna do?"

***

When the day finally ended, Dorothy was yelled at and cursed more times than she could count. Some of the residents had threatened to sue her, the property management company, and the building's owner. A few of them said they weren't going to pay their rent.

But most did.

In the office's lockbox were fourteen money orders and eight hundred dollars in cash.

She wasn't supposed to take the cash, but she had done it repeatedly over the years without telling Fred. The policy was to only accept cashier's checks or money orders. Dorothy took cash to make it easy on the residents. Even though it was opposed to corporate policy, that had always been her policy—to take care of her residents.

Just like Alma Moore, nine of the residents paid with money orders with uncompleted payee lines.

Dorothy separated the money orders into two piles. Those with the payee identified and those without. There was almost $4,100 in a stack without a payee identified. With the cash added, it was just short of $4,900.

She made out a deposit slip for the properly completed money orders and tucked the money into a deposit bag.

Then Dorothy slipped the pile of improperly filled-out money orders and cash into the receipt book and put it into the office safe.

Only she and Anita had the combination.

***

"Only seventeen hundred was deposited yesterday?" Fred Tresko asked. It was clear he was irritated.

"Yes," Dorothy said into the telephone. "I know."

"Today's the second. Usually, we have about seven grand deposited by now."

"People are upset by the eviction. Many have said they aren't going to pay."

"You make them pay," Fred angrily said. "What about the Lamplighter? Lester's our biggest tenant, and he always pays on the first."

"He said he wasn't paying."

Dorothy glanced at the safe. There were more money orders in there now that hadn't been filled out. More cash, too.

Fred said, "Lester didn't say any of that bullshit when I saw him."

"He was pretty upset about how you treated him."

"Fuck him. Tell him he has to pay."

"I did, and he said no."

"Tell him again." Even through the phone, she heard Fred pounding on his desk. "He owes us rent."

"What am I going to threaten him with?" Dorothy asked. "He's already being evicted."

Except for Fred's heavy breathing, the phone was silent for several seconds.

"I pay you for results," the property manager said. It was clear he was trying to control his anger. "I don't care how you do it but get that rent. The Lamplighter's, too."

Dorothy thought about Lester's comment about how when she no longer served a purpose to Fred Tresko, she would be on the street. He was closer to the truth than he knew.

"Are you still there?" Fred asked.

"Yeah."

"Why? You should be out collecting the rent."

Fred hung up before Dorothy could respond.

***

"There're a lot of angry people living in this building now," Earl said.

"I'm one of them," Dorothy said.

They were in the manager's office. Dorothy was filling out a deposit slip for a couple of cashier's checks that had the management company's name on them. Earl stood in front of the maintenance request basket and flipped through the slips of paper that had come in since the previous day.

"How long you staying around?" Earl asked.

"Today?"

"No. Here." Earl pointed at the floor. "Are you staying until they fire you?"

"What other choice do I have? I need the paycheck and the apartment. Besides, I need to take care of the people who live here."

He grunted.

"What?"

"We should quit," Earl said. "All of us. Fuck them before they can fuck us."

"Language, please."

"Sorry, but that don't make what I'm saying not true. We need to hit them where it hurts—the pocketbook. That's all rich people understand. Hit them in the wallet, they pay attention. You can't appeal to their… what's it called?"

"Sense of decency?"

"Right. You can't appeal to their decency 'cause they

ain't got none."

"How does our quitting hit them in the wallet?"

"They got to hire someone to get these people out. You think those Vietnamese or Haitians—"

"They're Dominicans. We don't have any Haitian families living with us."

He waved his hand. "Dominicans. Haitians. It's all the same."

"No, they're not."

"They're Cubans with worse food."

"Earl."

"What I'm saying is this. None of those foreign families are going to leave willingly. They like it here. Same for the junkies. Those sons of bitches are going to hide in every nook and cranny to avoid hitting the street. They know the score. When the bomb goes off, only the junkies and cockroaches will survive."

"Earl, the pocketbook?"

"Right. Without you, me, and Anita, what would that bastard Tresko do? He'd be up to his ass in alligators trying to get these people out in time. He'd have to spend a ton of money to hire emergency workers. He'd hate to do that."

Dorothy smirked. "He'd just bring someone over from another property. Fred will have contingency plans." She puffed out her cheeks. "Wished I would have thought ahead. I don't have a dime saved."

Earl tossed the maintenance requests back into the basket. "Well, don't be surprised if I fail to show up one day."

"You got some money saved up, Earl?"

The maintenance man smiled. "Of course, I do. I'm not as stupid as everyone makes me out to be."

***

By the fifth of the month, Dorothy had deposited nearly $6,000 in the bank. Another $4,000 had been sent directly to the property management office by social service agencies helping out tenants. That was only a portion of the rent that should have been collected by now—that had been collected.

Dorothy hid almost $18,000 of cash and unmarked money orders behind a refrigerator in a vacant apartment. She could no longer leave the money in the safe where Anita might see it or in the office where anyone would find it. She couldn't bear to take the money to her apartment—not yet at least. Doing that was the final act—a line she knew if she crossed, there would be no turning back from.

If the money remained inside the Hope, but not in her residence, Dorothy convinced herself she really hadn't done anything wrong.

That afternoon she sat before Fred Tresko to account for the lack of rent collection.

"You're twenty-two thousand outstanding," he said. He leaned forward and glared at her. "When are you bringing that in?"

"You don't know what it's like there," Dorothy said. "It's not a happy place."

"It's never been a happy place. Do your job. Get the rent."

"Nobody is worried about getting evicted for not paying."

"Play on their sympathies then. Tell them you can lose your job."

Her mouth fell open. "You'd fire me over this?"

Fred closed his eyes. "Of course not." When he

opened his eyes, he looked away. "I just said that as an example, you know, so you could say something to get them on your side. They like you."

Dorothy watched him.

"Do this for me," Fred's eyes closed again, "and I'll give you a bonus. The best bonus you've ever seen." When he opened his eyes, he smiled. "Okay?"

Dorothy looked away. "Okay." She wasn't any better at lying than he was.

***

When she returned to the Hope, Dorothy found two of the men who hadn't paid rent standing in a corner of the lobby. They appeared to be in the middle of an argument. One of the men, Joe, gesticulated wildly while he spoke. The other, Tom, crossed his arms and frowned. His head was cocked to the side as Joe prattled on.

She approached them and noticed their combined aroma from several feet away. They smelled as if they hadn't bathed in days. Both men had the quick, jerky spasms that many drug users develop.

Dorothy waited patiently for either man to notice her so she could interrupt their conversation. Neither glanced her way, though, and simply continued with their argument.

"I'm telling you," Joe said, insistently tapping his friend in the chest. "Britney is a fucking genius."

Tom reared back in mock horror. "The fuck is wrong with you? Saying shit like that."

"She's a pure pop powerhouse." Joe flicked the side of his mouth and made three popping sounds. "Tell me she's not. I dare you."

"She's not."

Joe threw his hands in the air. "You can't be serious. Who are you gonna say is better than the Holy Spearit?"

Tom's face scrunched. "Uh. I don't know. How about Taylor Sw—"

Joe slapped Tom.

Dorothy jumped at the sudden violence between the two friends. "Out!" she hollered. "You two out. Right now!"

Surprised to see her standing there, both men turned and said in unison, "What'd we do?"

"Out!" she repeated. She pushed and cajoled the men toward the door. They went unwillingly and made protesting noises until they were outside on the east stairs.

"There's no fighting in the Hope," she said.

Tom faced her with clasped hands. "Dorothy, hey now, I'm sorry. Me and Joe were only talking."

Joe laughed. "Until I slapped the living shit out of you."

Tom hit Joe then.

A donnybrook ensued that tumbled down the steps and onto the sidewalk where Vernon Brown had been enjoying a cigarette. The older man jumped out of the way and angrily flicked his cigarette at the two.

Dorothy pushed the door shut. "Stay out!" she hollered through the window.

She was halfway to her office before realizing she forgot to ask the two men about their rent.

***

Other than Joe and Tom, Dorothy tracked down the other non-payers. Some of them told her in the shortest way possible to do something anatomically impossible.

But four of them reluctantly handed her the rent they owed. One was in cash, and three were in money orders—two of those did not have a payee identified.

Dorothy returned to her office and opened the safe. She pulled out the receipt book and completed a receipt for the one resident who had properly completed her money order.

Then she hurried up to the third floor. Checking the hallway to make sure no one saw her at the door, she opened the vacant apartment and entered. She locked the door once inside. Behind the unplugged refrigerator, she found the envelope and pulled it out.

She added the cash to it as well as the two money orders. Then she tallied what was there. There was now over twenty thousand—enough for her to grab it and run. But she hesitated. She'd never stolen anything before. Not only was it against her upbringing. It was against the Bible. She didn't dare do it.

Don't be naïve, she thought. Twenty thousand isn't enough.

Dorothy closed the envelope and tucked it behind the refrigerator.

***

When she stepped into the bar, a waft of smoke billowed out. Some of it smelled like marijuana. While legal in the state, it wasn't permitted to smoke it inside a place like the Lamplighter.

Lester Poole stood behind the bar with a lit cigarette dangling from his mouth.

The door swung closed behind Dorothy as she stalked over to the bartender. "Lester."

Several patrons near them "Oohed" at the same time.

The bar owner removed the cigarette from his mouth then knocked its ash into a glass tray on the bar. "Yes?"

"You and these people—"

"*These* people?"

"—cannot smoke in here."

He stuck the cigarette back in his mouth. "Call the Health Department."

"Excuse me?"

"Let them come and take away my lighter. I'll go buy another."

Several of the patrons snickered.

Dorothy glanced around. "Can we…"

"Can we *what*?"

"Talk in private? Maybe someplace less smoky."

He jerked his head toward the front then turned to yell at the woman in the kitchen. "Chandra! Cover the bar."

Lester walked out the door with Dorothy close on his heels. When they were on the sidewalk, Lester leaned his shoulders against the building. "What's so important you gotta interrupt my business?"

"You need to pay your rent."

He jammed his tongue underneath his upper lip.

"I'm serious, Les."

"It's not happening."

"But you have a lease."

"A month-to-month contract isn't a lease; it's as worthless as a handshake."

"You made a deal."

"A deal? With the landlord, you mean? The lord of this land." He pointed at the sidewalk. "Having a lease makes it sound like me and her are partners, but I'm not her partner—am I? I'm her lackey, her servant, her—"

"Don't say it."

Lester scrunched his nose. "Out of respect, I won't,

but you know that's what I am in this situation—making her rich by breaking my back. Scraping by while she lives in some big house somewhere on the hill. The rich get richer. Remember last year when those white boys were knocking out those suits, making all that noise about the unfairness of the one percent? Starting to make some sense now, huh?"

Dorothy watched the passing traffic.

"You ever met her?" he asked.

She looked at Lester. "Mrs. Caldwell?"

"Missus Caldwell." Lester spat. "Even her name sounds rich. Arrogant. Missus Caldwell, would you like some tea? I bet there was a plantation in her family history."

"I've never met her."

"Never met her, yet you're doin' all this dirty work in her name. Puttin' all these people out of their homes, puttin' me out of my business. In the end, you'll be out of a job, and she'll be richer. You and me, we're the same in her eyes."

A city bus roared by. A wave of hot diesel exhaustion followed it and turned Dorothy's stomach.

Lester pushed off the wall. "You ever consider walkin' away? Just tell Fred Tresko to fuck himself?"

Dorothy shook her head.

He dropped his cigarette to the sidewalk and ground it out with the toe of his shoe. "I'd rather quit my job than help an asshole like Tresko oppress others to make a woman like Missus Caldwell richer." He faced her now, nose-to-nose. Dorothy could smell the cigarette on his breath. "Don't ask me for the rent no more. Got it? I'm never paying another dime for this place."

He turned and opened the door to the Lamplighter. Some funky music escaped the bar along with another plume of smoke.

***

"You've had enough time," Fred Tresko said. "It's time we do this."

Dorothy leaned forward. "But—"

"You were right. I didn't listen. There's nothing to threaten them with anymore. They know it, so we've got to act now."

She was at the Paulsen Center in the office of Sterling Management. Fred had called her over that morning. It was the eighth of the month.

He continued. "I'm going to move toward evictions on the lot who didn't pay. Lester included. We need to get them out now rather than later. Set an example if you will. If we don't, no one will believe we'll carry through with the evictions at the end of the month."

"What about attorney's fees?"

"It's a drop in the bucket for Mrs. Caldwell."

"I mean for the tenants. You'll bill them back."

Fred sniggered. "Of course, I'll bill them back. They should have thought about that before they withheld their rent. Besides, most of these folks will get out before we actually hire an attorney. Right now, we're only threatening. Lester will be the hard case. He'll probably hang around, but that old bastard will be fun to do some damage to. Maybe ruin his credit."

"When are you sending out the notices?"

Fred handed her a stack of three-day pay-or-quit warnings. "Don't worry about it. Just deliver these today."

Dorothy's hands shook, and she struggled to swallow.

"You okay?" he asked.

"Not really."

"Relax, Dorothy. It has to be done." Fred picked up the receiver of his phone. "They did this. Not us. This is on them. It's time to drop the hammer."

She left his office without another word.

***

Dorothy sat in the manager's office, reading one of the three-day notices she was to hand-deliver. It gave a delinquent resident three days to pay their rent or vacate their apartment. It showed exactly how much rent was due and the late fees that were now tacked on.

Late fees, she thought. Now, the resident who was late would be required to pay an additional charge. Her heart sunk.

The notice she held in her hand belonged to Alma Moore. Her money order was part of the collective pot hidden away behind the refrigerator. Now, reality set in for Dorothy.

Even if she refused to deliver these notices, the end was in sight. Fred would send the registered notices today and the non-paying tenants would receive them tomorrow.

As soon as Alma received that notice—not the one in her hand—the older woman would complain to the management office, and Dorothy would get caught.

Just holding onto a resident's rent for longer than twenty-four hours was cause for discipline, perhaps even termination. Even though the money never left the building, never entered Dorothy's apartment, she had stolen it. She was as guilty as if she'd left the property and gone to Tahiti.

Dorothy was so lost in her thoughts that she didn't

notice Earl Ricci enter the office.

"What're those?"

"Three-day notices."

"Serious?"

She nodded and put Alma's notice back on top of the stack.

"Fred's evicting folks who aren't payin' 'cause they're already being evicted?" Earl's voice rose while his face reddened. "What a prick. Someone should take that guy down a peg."

"If he doesn't get them out, the rest won't believe he'll do it at the end of the month." The words she parroted were pure Fred.

Earl slapped the wall. "Well, fuck that. And fuck him."

"*Earl.*"

"No, Dottie. I ain't watchin' my language. If there was ever a time for the F-word, it's now. Fuck this job. I don't need to work for a place like this. I got my integrity." He tapped his chest. "I quit."

He spun to leave and bumped into Anita, who had just entered the office. She fell against the wall. Earl reached for her, but she lifted her hands in surrender.

"I'm okay," she said.

Earl's face softened. "I'm real sorry, Anita. It was an accident."

Anita straightened. "What's going on in here?"

He thumbed over his shoulder. "Ask Dottie. I'm outta here." Earl hurried away then. The hammer hanging from his tool belt slapped against his leg.

When he disappeared around the corner, Anita raised her eyebrows in a questioning manner.

"Earl quit," Dorothy said.

"Over what?"

"Three-days."

Anita canted her head. "Pay or quits? This month?"

"Yeah."

Anita's face scrunched. "Who hasn't paid?" She picked up the top notice. "Alma Moore? But I thought she came in already."

Dorothy couldn't look Anita in the eyes.

"This doesn't make any sense." Anita's voice was soft.

"None of it makes sense," Dorothy said.

"You're right." The paper slid from Anita's hand back to the desk. "I'm going for a drink."

"You've been drinking a lot lately."

"And?"

Dorothy shrugged.

"Write me up."

"Why would I do that?"

"Yeah. Why would you?"

Dorothy met her eyes then. "Mind if I join you?"

"You want a morning libation?"

"Seems a good day for one. I'll meet you over there."

Anita eyed the notices before leaving. It seemed as if she wanted to say something, but then she left.

With Anita gone, Dorothy leaned back in her chair, turned her head, and stared at the safe. She thought about collecting the money she had hidden and putting it in there.

Maybe she could tuck it into a corner and pretend she hadn't seen it. But she'd already told Fred the tenants hadn't paid. Those she'd kept the money from were about to get notified the main office never received their payments.

Dorothy started this ball rolling, and now she was about to get crushed by it.

***

When she pulled the door to the Lamplighter open, it was dark inside, and some music she vaguely remembered from her youth played softly.

Anita was at the bar with a clear drink in her hand. Lester Poole was at the opposite end serving another customer. Even though it was still the morning, the place already seemed busy.

When Dorothy sat on a stool, Anita said, "So, I've been thinking."

"About?"

"Those notices."

Dorothy faced her.

Anita sipped her drink. "Some of those tenants are gonna be real upset to find they're being evicted early—especially after they already paid."

"But they haven't," Dorothy said.

"If that's gonna be your story, best stick to it, but you better be more convincing than that." Anita shot her a sideways glance. "I talked with Alma. She told me she paid. How many others in that stack will say the same?"

Dorothy did her best to appear calm.

Lester sauntered over. "Drinking with us today?"

"She ain't stayin'," Anita said.

Dorothy remained silent, but Lester asked, "She ain't?"

"Nope."

"She's sittin' like she is."

"Dottie's got to get back to the office," Anita said. "Ain't that right?"

"Yeah," Dorothy said. "Gotta get back."

Anita continued. "She's got things to straighten out."

Lester's eyes narrowed. "Another time then."

"Another time," Anita agreed.

The bartender walked to the far end of the bar.

Dorothy whispered, "Anita, what did I do to you?"

Anita's face hardened. "You act like a mother hen, but when the chips are down, you're about to do worse to these people than the one who's evicting them. You're not their friend."

Dorothy lowered her head.

"Don't sit there looking all remorseful. I didn't do this. Go clean up your mess unless you want me to handle it for you."

Her head snapped up.

"I can call Fred and tell him what I think is going on. That'll solve the problem."

Dorothy slid off her stool and took an awkward step back. She held on to the edge of the bar to steady herself. As bravely as she could, she said, "Don't bother coming in for the rest of the day."

Anita raised her empty drink and shook it. "I wouldn't think of it."

***

Dorothy sat on the vacant apartment floor and counted the cash and unmarked money orders in the envelope. This was what her integrity was worth.

She put the money into her pocket, went back to her office, and called Fred Tresko. She didn't exactly know what she would say to the man when he answered, but she'd tell the truth.

He answered on the third ring, "Fred Tresko."

"It's Dorothy."

"You get those eviction notices out yet?"

The stack of them still sat on her desk.

"About those."

"Don't tell me you're having second thoughts about doing your job."

"No, no, that's not it."

"Because if you need me to come down there and do it for you, I will." She didn't like his tone. "We don't have time to screw around with these people."

"I'm just running behind, is all."

"Then get them out."

She rubbed the cross around her neck. "Yeah, okay."

He hung up on her.

Dorothy picked up the stack of three-day notices and returned to the vacant apartment on the third floor. Carefully, she hid the envelope behind the refrigerator. She put the yellow warnings inside the fridge then locked up the empty unit.

Then she went to her apartment. She was taking a mental health day.

What was Fred going to do? Fire her?

***

Anita's words had rung in Dorothy's head all night, and she finally decided she couldn't live with a lifetime of guilt. In the morning, she checked into the office shortly before seven. There were no new voice mails and no work orders to review. After making sure Earl Ricci had not returned to work, she hurried back to the vacant apartment. She collected the envelope of undeposited rents along with the undelivered notices.

Upon returning to the manager's office, she pulled the rents from the envelope and tossed them haphazardly into the safe. Then she threw the stack of pay-or-quit notices into the trash can.

She dialed Fred's phone and waited for his voicemail. Dorothy wanted to call him before the office opened so there would be no chance for the man to pick up. When the voicemail eventually started, she waited to leave her message.

"Hi, Fred, it's Dorothy. A couple things. First, I found those missing rent payments. They'd fallen behind the safe. Yeah, so, everybody's caught up. Well, almost everybody. A couple of the boys are still behind, but you know how they are. I'll get after them."

She cringed with how she sounded. Her story was stupid and simple, and it made no sense. Her only hope was Fred would be happy the money was found.

"When the banks open later," she continued, "I'll process the payments and deposit them. Okay, that's all I wanted to let you know. I'm going to get something to eat now, and I'll be back in a bit. Have a good morning."

She started to hang up the phone when she said, "Oh, yeah, and Earl quit. He was pretty upset about the three-days. So, we don't have a maintenance man around. Not sure how you want me to handle requests until the end of the month. We can talk about that later."

When she finished, she hung up the phone and stared at it.

The mail usually wouldn't arrive until shortly before noon. At that point, residents who had received the three-day notices in the mail would call her to complain, or they would call the main office to find out why their rent payments hadn't been applied to their accounts. Dorothy would need to get the payments to the bank as soon as possible. That way, when the residents called, she would have a reasonable excuse it was all just a mix-up.

That sounded plausible. Happy with her plan, Dorothy

grabbed her purse and left the office. First, she wanted some breakfast.

The banks weren't open until nine, anyway.

***

The egg and sausage biscuit was hot when she bit into it. She chewed for a moment before sipping her coffee to wash it down. The brown liquid burned her tongue. She clenched her jaw and tightened her lips. She took a long, breath through her nose.

Why had she tried to steal the money? she wondered. She wasn't that type of person. What made her think she could get away with it, let alone live with herself after stealing? Temptation was a powerful thing. She'd been lucky to break free of it before it ruined her life. She'd seen so many lives destroyed by uncontrolled impulses.

Her body began to shake then the tears started. She had never stolen anything in her life, and she was too old to start.

Anita was right. For years, Dorothy acted as a mother to the Hope residents, and now, when push came to shove, she considered stealing from them. What kind of person would do that? She was ashamed of herself.

The tears continued for several minutes until she realized several patrons were watching her. A concerned employee walked over.

"Is everything okay, ma'am?"

She nodded. "I'll be fine. Sorry. Bad morning."

The employee, a young woman with kind eyes, touched her shoulder. "Let me know if you need anything."

Dorothy looked down into her coffee as she absently rubbed the cross hanging around her neck.

***

Outside the restaurant, the morning sun shone on Dorothy. She smiled as it warmed her face. In a moment of self-affirmation, she proclaimed, "I'm not a criminal."

"Why'n the hell not?" a man sitting on the sidewalk asked.

Dorothy stared at him, and he extended a hand.

"Got a dollar?"

She gave him the change from her breakfast order.

As she walked back to the Hope, she figured she needed to apologize to Anita. She owed it to her friend for helping her see that she had been about to make a mistake. When Dorothy rounded the corner on Madison, she stopped.

Two police cars were parked in front of the building. Dorothy picked up her pace.

As she neared the east entrance, Vernon Brown moved away from the door. "Sorry, Dorothy."

"It's okay," she said and dismissively waved at the cigarette in his hand.

Vernon didn't seem too concerned about smoking near the Hope. Instead, his eyes were on the front door and what might be occurring inside. She hurried up the stairs and yanked open the door. Two officers stood near her office. Dorothy hurried through the lobby toward them.

"Can I help you?" she asked.

The first officer turned to her. He was a young man with a genial demeanor. His blue nametag read *Sutton*. "Ma'am?"

As the officer stepped aside, Dorothy saw Fred Tresko sitting behind her desk with the door to the safe open. The stack of pay-or-quit notices were now on the corner of her desk.

"Come in, Dorothy. We've been waiting for you."

"What's going on?"

"There's been a theft," Fred said.

"A theft?" Dorothy asked. She looked at the first officer and then to the older officer whose nametag read *McCrea*. They both stared back at her. "Of what?"

"Rent money," Fred said.

"But it's all in there." Dorothy pointed at the safe. "Well, except a couple boys, but I figured we'd talk about those."

The property manager leaned over and swung the safe's door fully open. It was empty inside.

Dorothy inhaled. Where had the carelessly thrown money orders and dollar bills gone?

Fred frowned and shook his head. "It's not your fault, Dorothy."

"It's not?"

He looked from her to the officers. "How were you to know Earl would do something like this?"

"Earl didn't steal the rent money."

"He quit, right?"

"Well, yes."

"You said he was pretty angry over the three-day notices."

"We all were."

"I got a message from a resident last night who said she paid her rent a week ago."

Dorothy suddenly felt light-headed. "The mail already came?"

"We mailed the notices two days ago. I waited for you to hand-deliver them, so they'd get them on the same day."

Fred's eyes searched hers and she did her best to stay

calm. Her mouth was dry, and she struggled to swallow.

"Alma Moore," Fred said. "Lady left a heckuva message—a real earful. I figured it must have been a mistake. Then I heard your voicemail. That's why I ran down here right away. I saw the receipts inside but no money. I knew you wouldn't have taken the money without the receipts. That's not how you work. Anita neither. Maybe Earl, right?"

Dorothy glanced to the two officers who watched her closely.

"What about this Anita?" Officer McCrea asked.

"No, she's in the clear," Fred said. "She called me last night."

"Anita?" Dorothy croaked.

"She wanted to talk about the rents, too."

Dorothy swayed slightly. "She did?"

Fred nodded. "Did you know she drank during the day? We probably should talk about that. Liability issues and all."

Dorothy nodded. "What did she say?"

"I don't know. She was so messed up, I told her we would talk today."

"Oh," Dorothy said.

"After I got your message, I figured she was calling to leave the same you did. That the money was found. You two must have talked."

"Yeah," Dorothy muttered.

Fred glanced toward the safe. "You didn't take the money, did you, Dorothy?"

"I didn't take it," she blurted. Dorothy fought the urge to look back at the policemen. Instead, she stared at Fred. "The money was in the safe. I promise."

"That's what I figured. So, it must be Earl, right?"

Nothing made sense to Dorothy. Earl didn't have the

combination to the safe. Only she and Anita had it. So, maybe Anita took the money while Dorothy was at breakfast and left her holding the bag for the theft. That didn't seem like something she would do, especially after the scolding she gave Dorothy at the Lamplighter.

"So, Earl?" Fred prompted. "Am I right about him or what?"

"I don't know," Dorothy mumbled and lowered her head.

What else could she say with the two policemen standing there? Pointing the finger at Anita would be like pointing the finger at herself.

Officer McCrea said, "Has anything been stolen or not?"

Fred eyed Dorothy. "Why don't you fellas give us a couple minutes until we can figure this whole mess out?"

The policeman thumbed toward the lobby. "We'll be out front. Let us know when you come to a decision."

When the officers left, Dorothy turned back to Fred. She didn't want to tell him about her suspicions regarding Anita. She couldn't believe her friend would steal the money, yet only the two of them had the combination. There was no way Earl could have taken the money.

As Dorothy stared into the open safe, her eyes slanted. She cast a sideways glance to Fred. He watched her with mild curiosity.

"You took the money," she said.

"Me?" he said.

She pointed at the safe. "You have the combination, too. You're the one who gave it to us."

Fred closed his eyes. "I didn't take it."

"You're lying."

"How can you say that?"

She swallowed before saying, "You close your eyes

when you lie.”

Fred folded his arms over his belly. “I do?”

“Ever since I’ve known you. Yes, you do.”

“You never told me?”

She shook her head.

“Glad we don’t play poker, or you could have taken me for a lot of money.”

“I should tell the police it was you.”

“Where’s your proof?”

Dorothy glared at him.

“Besides, it was you who held it back.”

“The money never left the property,” Dorothy said, “and I put it back.”

“Holding the money and not depositing it shows intent of theft. The fact is the money isn’t here now.” Fred pointed at the empty safe. “Two plus two. Since you don’t know where the money is…” He widened his eyes and lifted his hands. “Oops. Doesn’t matter. That still equals four. Do you know what Anita told me?”

Her face flattened.

“That’s right. We talked. She was drunk as a skunk and let loose on you. Phew. Boy, was she mad. Called you a crook.”

Dorothy held onto the back of a chair. She felt lightheaded.

“Anita said you stole the missing rent payments. I was planning to confront you this morning, but then you left that voicemail. You must have been all torn up inside, so I ran down here to see the money for myself.”

“I knew it,” Dorothy whispered.

“I called the police, so I think I have a little better alibi than you. However, feel free to grab those officers and let’s tell your side of the story. Then we’ll talk to all the residents who paid their rent to you. And we’ll talk to

Anita, who told me about her suspicions. Then we'll ask the cops what they think."

"You have the money."

"Again, where's your proof?"

Dorothy's lip trembled.

"All you got to do is play it smart, Dorothy, and I'll give you a thousand dollars. We'll blame it on Earl. Or Anita. Hell, make it Lester's fault, for all I care. You pick. We won't tell the cops. That'll be another one of our secrets."

She cocked her head. "Why are you doing this?"

"What do you mean why? There's twenty grand at stake, plus the thrill of getting away with it. Why were you doing it?"

"Because I was out of a job."

Fred closed his eyes. "I told you I would take care of you." His eyes popped open. "I did it again, didn't I?"

She nodded.

"Son of a bitch."

Dorothy's gaze drifted over several pictures of her, Anita, and Earl that hung on the walls. The three of them were at various functions held by Sterling Management. They were often standing together with big smiles.

She faced Fred now. "You won't tell the cops?"

He stood. "It's hard to get away with anything if we tell the truth."

"In that case," she said, "I want half."

He nodded several times. When he finally decided on a course of action, he held out his hand, and Dorothy shook it. Fred Tresko never closed his eyes when he said, "You've got a deal, Dorothy Givens."

She smiled and breathed a sigh of relief.

Officer Safety

The yellow Toyota Tundra raced through the red light at Spokane Falls Boulevard and turned north onto Ruby Street. The pickup narrowly avoided hitting a newer Lexus as it careened through the last intersection on the edge of downtown. It fishtailed into the furthest of the three northbound lanes on Ruby. When the Toyota straightened its course, it sideswiped an early '70s Volkswagen Beetle. The little orange car lurched away from the middle lane.

Officer Lucas Jefferson sped through the corner in pursuit. His patrol car's engine revved in protest as he accelerated. Above him, emergency lights flicked between red and blue. A siren wailed its warning into the night.

"Out of the way!" Jefferson yelled as the Lexus drifted to the side of the road.

In the passenger seat of the patrol car, Officer Ron Rowe keyed his microphone. "David-435, northbound on Ruby."

The two men were using Jefferson's callsign that night since he'd logged them into the car.

"*Copy, four-thirty-five,*" the dispatcher said. "*Channel is still restricted. Lieutenant is now monitoring the call.*"

"Better hurry," Rowe said.

The engine revved louder and Jefferson pounded the steering wheel. "He's gonna terminate the pursuit!"

Rowe pointed at the Volkswagen. "Pay attention!"

"What do you think I'm doing?"

The orange Beetle overcorrected and shot into their

lane. Jefferson jerked the steering wheel to the left and immediately back to the right. The patrol car whipped around the little car.

Up ahead, the Toyota weaved in and out of the Friday night traffic. It was nearly midnight. The colleges hadn't yet let out for the summer so traffic this time of night was active. The downtown bars were still jammed, and it was too early for the high school kids to be home.

"Move!" shouted Jefferson. He angrily waved his free hand back and forth.

A minivan lurched to the side of the road and the patrol car zoomed by. The female driver scowled at them as they passed.

"David-four-thirty-five, advise of speed and conditions."

"He's gonna do it," Jefferson said with a shake of his head. "What did I tell you?"

Rowe leaned over and glanced at the speedometer. He activated the microphone. "Four-thirty-five, speed is seventy-four." He sat upright. "Road is dry. Traffic is moderate."

"Four-thirty-five, any other PC for pursuit?"

"Are you kidding?" Jefferson shouted. "It's fucking stolen and used in a robbery!"

Rowe waggled the microphone in the direction of his partner. "You done?"

Further up the road, the Toyota Tundra swerved widely onto a side street.

Jefferson zoomed around a slow-moving Buick that refused to move to the side of the road.

Rowe keyed the microphone. "Four-thirty-five. We've also got PC for hit and run, reckless driving, and—"

"Terminate pursuit," the dispatcher announced.

"But we can get Pierre!" Jefferson hollered.

"All units, slow down. Pursuit is terminated. Channel is unrestricted."

Rowe faced his partner. "Slow down." Into the microphone, he said, "David-435, copy. Terminating pursuit." Once again to Jefferson, Rowe dejectedly said, "Slow down."

The engine stopped whining and the car coasted to a slower speed.

Rowe silenced the siren before clicking off the emergency flashers.

The dispatcher called out the particulars of Macon Pierre, the suspect behind the wheel of the truck. She also provided the plate number and another description of the pickup.

But Lucas Jefferson wasn't listening. Instead, he smacked the wheel with the palm of his hand. "That lieutenant."

"Next time."

Jefferson shook his head. "Dickless wonder."

"We knew the driver. What'd you expect?"

They turned onto Desmet Avenue. It was a natural desire to follow the path the truck had taken. In the middle of the road was the Toyota Tundra. It had collided with an Audi and blocked the roadway. Parked cars lined both sides of the street. The driver's door of the pickup was open, and Macon Pierre was gone. The driver of the Audi was climbing out of his car.

"He's out," Jefferson said excitedly.

"Stop!" Rowe hollered as he jumped from the patrol car and jogged over to the Audi driver.

Jefferson snatched the microphone from its holder. "David-435."

"Four-thirty-five?"

The driver gesticulated wildly to Rowe and brought

his hands together to simulate a crash.

"Four-thirty-five, our suspect has collided with a vehicle at Desmet and Ruby. Medics are not required. And?"

The driver pointed east then slapped his hands. Jefferson knew what the driver was telling his partner. Rowe faced Jefferson and thumbed over his shoulder.

"Four-thirty-five, go ahead."

Officer Ron Rowe turned and ran eastbound.

"Four-thirty-five, Pierre's fled on foot. Eastbound on Desmet. David-436 is out of the car. We're gonna see if we can find him."

"Four-thirty-five, copy."

The Mobile Data Computer next to Jefferson's elbow beeped multiple times. He didn't check what was occurring because he already knew. Other units joined his call, but they stayed off the air in case Rowe needed to jump back on with an update.

Jefferson activated the emergency flashers again, dropped his car into gear, and reversed onto Ruby Street. Once he was clear of the corner, he popped the gearshift into Drive, and raced ahead two blocks to Sharp Avenue. He figured that was far enough to—

"Four-thirty-six," Rowe called. *"Foot pursuit!"*

Jefferson turned eastbound onto Sharp Avenue.

"Northbound on Pearl, approaching Boone." Rowe's voice was strong, but the exertion of running was evident.

"Channel is restricted for David-four-thirty-six," the dispatcher announced.

Jefferson's patrol car accelerated as it raced along Sharp. He tapped the brakes before spinning the wheel to the right. The tires protested the physics of the turn, but the car eventually straightened and propelled him southbound.

Macon Pierre was a tall, thin white male with scraggly long hair. He wore jeans and Doc Martens, but no shirt. He sprinted northbound. Behind him but gaining ground was Ron Rowe.

Jefferson jammed the brakes and skidded the patrol car to a stop. He shoved the gearshift into Park, jumped out, and moved to the front of the car.

Pierre was trapped between two buildings. There was no escape route. He had to go through Jefferson or turn around and run back toward Rowe.

The tall white man lowered his head and kicked like a fullback sprinting for the endzone.

Lucas Jefferson hunched, took a couple of gauging steps, then hit Macon Pierre in the midsection just like his college football coach had taught him—head to the side, shoulder tucked in, arms wrapped around the midsection. It was designed to keep both players safe.

Unfortunately, it had been years since Jefferson tackled anyone like that.

***

Macon Pierre stood in front of the patrol car with his hands cuffed. His long hair hung in front of his face. Some of it was matted to his forehead due to sweat. Tattoos covered his bare chest. Over his left breast was a swastika. On the other breast, a circle and a cross were in the middle of flames. Across his flat stomach were the words *White Devil*.

Lucas Jefferson and Ron Rowe stood nearby. Jefferson rubbed his aching shoulder while his partner shook his head.

Corporal Tom Clary lowered his camera. "One of you guys, pull his hair back so I can see his face."

A single eye peered through Pierre's matted hair. "Not the boo."

Jefferson cocked his head.

Rowe touched his partner's arm. "I got it. Besides, I've got gloves on."

Macon Pierre lifted his chin toward the night sky as Rowe brushed the hair away from his face. When he lowered his head, an abrasion was seen on the arrested man's left cheek.

"How bad is it?" Pierre asked.

"Barely a scratch," Clary said.

"Hurts worse than that." Pierre clucked his tongue and glanced at Jefferson. "Lucky you had your backup."

"Yeah?" Jefferson asked.

"Look at the camera," the corporal said.

Pierre curled his lip and continued to glare at Jefferson.

"This is for you, Pierre," Corporal Clary said. "If you don't want me to document your injuries, I'm happy to go about my day."

The arrested man faced Clary. "Why didn't you say so? Want me to smile?"

Clary lifted the camera. "Do what you like."

Pierre grinned. Blood covered his teeth.

"Turn to the right," the corporal said.

Pierre faced Jefferson. "I owe you, bunny."

"Keep talking," Jefferson said.

"When you least expect it."

The camera flashed.

"Let me see the other side," the corporal said.

Pierre sneered at Jefferson. "Trust me. It's coming."

Rowe chuckled. "Big talk for a man in handcuffs."

Pierre eyed Rowe. "He your boyfriend? Is that why you defend him?"

"Shut up," the corporal ordered, "and let me see the other side."

"I'll fuck you up, too," Pierre said to Rowe.

"Last chance," the corporal said, "or I'm done."

The suspect slowly turned. "They were rough on me, Sarge. I want that in your report."

"He's a corporal," Rowe said, "And you shouldn't have resisted."

"I didn't resist."

Rowe tapped his chest. "Tell that to my body camera. You don't think I wear this because I want to."

Another flash of the camera.

"Now," Clary said. "Let me see your back."

Pierre shuffled around. On his right shoulder was a large rash.

Corporal Clary leaned in with the camera and snapped a picture. He examined the screen then shook his head in frustration. "Ron, put your finger next to the abrasion."

Rowe eyed his partner.

"That's right," Pierre said. He spoke to Clary's reflection in the windshield. "Make sure you get a good picture for my lawsuit, Sarge. Ol' boo is gonna lose his badge. I think he broke my ribs, too."

"If he did," Rowe said, "you wouldn't be talking." He tapped his chest near the body camera. "You know I'm still recording this, right?" He jerked his head toward Jefferson. "Him, too."

Neither officer was recording now.

"What do I care?" Pierre said. "Boo is a term of endearment."

"Sure it is," Jefferson said. "I feel all warm and fuzzy every time you say it."

The corporal looked over the viewfinder at Rowe. "Ron, please."

Reluctantly, Rowe stepped toward the long-haired man and pointed to the abrasion on his shoulder.

The camera flashed.

Pierre laughed. "Cha-ching, baby."

***

"White lives matter."

Lucas Jefferson glanced over his left shoulder and winced from the pain. "Don't start."

"Hey, man." Macon Pierre scooted awkwardly across the plastic-covered backseat. It squeaked as he moved. Scooching anywhere in the tight confines of the rear seat was a difficult task as Pierre's hands remained cuffed behind his back. His face hovered near the Plexiglass shield that separated the passengers. Pierre's attention remained locked on the passenger. "Fuck your black lives."

From behind the steering wheel, Ron Rowe glanced into the rearview mirror. Pierre's eyes were again hidden behind a swath of long hair that had fallen in front of his face. "He said shut up."

Pierre continued. "Your lives aren't any more special than ours."

Jefferson didn't respond. Instead, he rubbed his shoulder.

"I hope you popped that out of its socket."

Rowe flicked on the radio and turned it up. Whoever was last in the car had it tuned to a country music channel. A song about calling the po-po filled the car.

"Oh yeah," Pierre exclaimed. "Five-one-five-oh," he sang out.

Jefferson flicked it off and the car went silent.

"Turn it back. That was my jam."

Rowe's eyes went to the rearview mirror. "Five-oh is already here, dumbass."

"Oh, you want some of this, too?" Pierre jerked his head to flick his hair from his face. He then looked in the rearview mirror to catch Rowe's attention. "You two a couple butt buddies or what? Always coming to his protection." He spat on the protective shield. "That's what I think of that."

"Sit back," Jefferson said.

Pierre dropped into his seat. That only lasted for a few seconds. He returned to his position next to the Plexiglass divider and craned his neck to look at Jefferson. "You think you can double dip? Blue lives matter, too? Fuck that. You're no better than us." Pierre hocked a loogie onto the Plexiglass this time. "There's more where that came from."

Rowe tapped the brakes and the car jerked as if stopping. Pierre's face slammed into the Plexiglass divider. The car accelerated quickly again, and Pierre was tossed backward into his seat.

Jefferson glanced over his shoulder which caused a twinge of pain in his shoulder. He winced.

"Jesus!" Pierre's face scrunched with obvious pain. "What was that?"

"A cat," Rowe muttered.

"Cat, my ass." Pierre looked up at the roof of the car and blinked several times. "You did that on purpose."

"It was a cat," Rowe insisted.

Pierre's face pinched and relaxed several times. "You guys need seatbelts back here. It's not safe."

Rowe glanced into the rearview mirror. "Next time, maybe listen. That's safe."

"There wasn't no cat."

"Sure, there was."

"Yeah?" Pierre stared at the ceiling. "Did you hit it?"

Jefferson eyed his partner then faced the man in the backseat. "No. He missed it."

"I wasn't talking to you, boo." Pierre awkwardly sat up and scooted forward again. He moved to within inches of the Plexiglass again. He tilted his head so he could see Jefferson. "Hey, tell me something. What's it like being a fly in a bowl full of rice?"

Rowe tapped the brakes again. Pierre's face slammed into the separation shield once more. When the car accelerated, the suspect flopped into his seat. "Jesus!"

Jefferson turned to see Pierre. His shoulder hurt doing so, but he fought back the grimace.

Pierre lay on the back seat. His face repeatedly squeezed and relaxed. "What the fuck, man?"

"Dog," said Rowe.

"There wasn't no dog!" Pierre shouted.

"Sure, there was."

Jefferson settled into his seat.

"I know what you're doing!" Pierre hollered. "I'm gonna have your badge. Both of—"

Rowe tapped the brakes and the car lurched forward once more. There was a thud in the backseat. Jefferson turned to look.

Pierre had slid off the plastic covered seats and now lay on the floorboard. He cried out in discomfort.

"Sorry about that," Rowe said. "Cats and dogs are running wild tonight. It's pandemonium."

Pierre struggled to get himself back into the seat. After a moment, he gave up. "I think I'll stay here until we get to jail."

"Probably a good idea," Jefferson said. His attention returned to the road ahead. "Safety first."

***

In the sally port of the Spokane County Jail, Jefferson and Rowe exited the patrol car and moved to the gun-secure station. Jefferson put his Glock into a small locker and removed the key. Rowe did the same.

Jefferson held out his hand to stop his partner from returning to their car. Inside, Macon Pierre still lay on the floorboard.

"What was that about?" Jefferson whispered.

"What?"

"The brake checks."

Rowe flicked his hand toward the car. "He wouldn't shut up."

"But the corporal already checked him at the scene for the use of force. What if he's got a broken nose or a black eye?"

"He doesn't."

"But what if?"

"He *doesn't.*"

The two men returned to the patrol car. They opened the back door and pulled Pierre from the floorboard. They were careful to make sure he didn't bump his head on the way out. When Pierre stood, he turned and angrily shouted, "I'm gonna have your badges!"

"We've heard it before," Rowe said.

"Then I'm gonna kill your wives!"

Rowe pointed to a camera in the lobby. "Say that again. They might not have heard you."

He tugged on Pierre's elbow and escorted him into the jail lobby. Jefferson remained behind and flipped up the backseat. This was always done to ensure an arrestee hadn't dumped anything they might have missed during a search incident to arrest.

Jefferson didn't find anything. He slapped the seat into place and went into the lobby.

***

Inside the harsh lights of the booking lobby, Lucas Jefferson studied Macon Pierre. The man's nose twitched as blood trickled from it. Bruising appeared to be forming around his left eye. He worried Rowe's brake checks were going to haunt them.

Deputy Sheriff Jerry Brasch read from his clipboard. Attached to it was the in-processing checklist. "Any allergies, diseases, or medical conditions?"

"They assaulted me."

Brasch looked up with a bored expression.

"With their car." Pierre glanced at the two officers, then to the deputy. "Aren't you gonna do something about it?"

The deputy raised his eyebrows. "They hit you with their car?"

"No. I was inside, but they—"

Brasch cleared his throat. "Any allergies, diseases, or medical conditions?"

"You don't believe me?"

The deputy looked up. The bored expression had returned.

Pierre's eyes narrowed. "I see how it is. You fuckers are all the same."

"Do I need to repeat my question?"

"No."

"Well?"

Pierre leaned his shoulders against a nearby wall. "I got a peanut allergy."

Brasch made a note on the checklist. "Peanut."

"And I'm lactose intolerant."

The deputy looked up from his clipboard. "For real?"

"Like I would joke about that. So what if I can't drink milk?" Pierre lifted his chin in the direction of the deputy's clipboard. "Write it down. I need a special diet."

Rowe and Jefferson chuckled.

Pierre glared at them. "That shit ain't funny."

Brasch frowned as he jotted the note on the clipboard.

"And I got diverticulitis, too."

"How do you spell that?" the deputy asked.

"Do I look like a doctor? You need to know this shit. Not me."

Rowe moved toward the deputy. "It's probably better if you ask what he doesn't have. For the master race, he seems pretty fragile."

Pierre rested the back of his head against the wall. "And I got a headache." Pierre looked down his nose at Brasch. "I think I got a concussion from the beating they gave me."

"We didn't give you a beating," Rowe said.

"Maybe it came from those cats and dogs running wild." Pierre looked to the deputy. "I wanna see the nurse. I know my rights."

Brasch cocked his head. "You're serious?"

"I think I might pass out from the pain."

Rowe stepped toward Pierre. "You stole a truck and robbed a family business." He pointed outside. "There are still cops out there investigating the collisions you caused, and you got the balls to cry about having a headache?"

"I think I got a busted rib, too."

Rowe lifted his hands in frustration. "Unbelievable."

Jefferson watched as a smile grew on Macon Pierre's face.

Sergeant Gene Summerhill crossed his arms and studied both Lucas Jefferson and Ron Rowe. He stood a few inches over six feet with thick arms and a bushy mustache.

They were in the parking lot of an office supply store on North Division. All three men stood in front of the sergeant's unmarked patrol car. It was almost three in the morning. Traffic had thinned noticeably on the arterial.

"So he fought with you?" Summerhill asked.

"He resisted," Rowe said, "but he didn't fight."

The sergeant eyed Jefferson. "You tackled him, though?"

"That's right. Like they taught in college." Jefferson patted his left shoulder. Doing so brought a twinge of pain, but he kept his face flat.

"Were your cameras activated?" Summerhill asked.

Both Rowe and Jefferson nodded.

"The camera in the car, too," Jefferson said. "The takedown should be on there."

"It was beautiful," Rowe said. "Luke brought him down like Brian Urlacher in his prime."

"I'd have gone with Mike Singletary." Jefferson hunched in a pre-snap linebacker pose. "But thanks for the compliment."

Summerhill frowned. "This is serious, you two. Anything else I need to know?"

Rowe and Jefferson eyed each other before both shaking their heads.

"The jail nurse gave Pierre a onceover," the sergeant said.

Rowe shrugged. "He was crying about a headache

before we left. So what?"

"So what?" Summerhill asked. "I got a heads up from the jail sergeant that he's pretty banged up."

"He got some road rash from the resisting," Jefferson said. "Hell, my shoulder is so screwed right now I can't get my arm above my head." He lifted his arm to show the limited range of motion. "Nobody's crying for me."

Summerhill lifted his chin. "Want to go to the ER?"

Jefferson shook his head. "I'll sleep it off and see how it is later."

"If it's not better, go to the doctor. We'll fill out an on-the-job injury report. Probably should do it anyway."

Rowe pointed at the sergeant. "What he said."

Summerhill watched a tricked-out Honda race southbound. Its engine rattled into the night. When it was out of earshot, he continued. "The jail staff photographed Pierre's injuries and the nurse is completing her report now."

Jefferson shoved his hands into his pockets. "We had Corporal Clary document Pierre's scuffs at the scene. They weren't that bad, all things considered."

"I know. Clary told me."

"There you go," Rowe said.

"He also said there wasn't a black eye and bloody nose."

Both officers remained silent.

Summerhill took a deep breath and held it. "I don't know what happened in the car, but it's time for you to write a report like your jobs depend upon it."

"Pierre isn't going to do anything," Rowe said. "His type never do."

"Until they do," Summerhill said. "You know the drill. Paper beats everything. It's more important than anything you do out on the street. Find a quiet place now and write your report. Detail exactly why you had to stop suddenly."

Jefferson and Rowe stared at the sergeant.

He frowned. "You two geniuses didn't invent the brake checks. So, what was it? A squirrel?"

"Dog," Rowe said.

Jefferson nodded.

"Did you tell Pierre that?"

"We did."

Jefferson eyed his partner. "We also told him about the cat."

"You did two?" Summerhill asked excitedly. "Christ, what were you thinking?" The sergeant put his hands on his hips. "It's always fun and games until someone gets sued." He turned away for a moment then quickly faced them. Summerhill pointed at each officer. "I've told you both this more than once—report writing is an officer safety skill. Tonight, you better treat it as such."

Sergeant Summerhill climbed into his car and drove southbound on Division.

Ron Rowe eyed his partner. "Yeah. I probably went too far."

Lucas Jefferson shrugged. "Too late for that now. Let's write the reports. There'll be no reason to worry after that."

Prologue to Disorder

Detective James Morgan dropped his car into gear and entered traffic. The Dodge Charger's engine roared as it raced southbound along Monroe Street toward the bridge. It was noon on an August Friday, so downtown would be busy.

In the passenger seat sat Detective Nayla Senai. She looked up from her cell phone as they zoomed by the courthouse. "Where are we headed?"

"You hungry?"

"I can eat."

Morgan changed lanes to speed around a slow-moving Porsche Cayenne. He tapped his brakes to avoid a truck up ahead, then dove back in ahead of the little European SUV.

He glanced at Senai. "We need to generate some arrests."

"Why are you looking at me?"

"I said we."

Senai made a face. "Uh-huh. What about the rest of the team?"

"Them, too. Our numbers are down this quarter."

"It's only half over. There's almost another full month to go."

"But the captain is whining, which means the lieutenant will fall over himself to stick a foot up the sergeant's ass."

Senai studied Morgan. "So, you're saying?"

"We've got to get creative."

"Like what? Make up stuff?"

He smirked. "That's not what I'm saying. I'll think of something. What're you in the mood for?"

"We're back to food?"

"Yeah."

She dropped her attention to her phone. "Then a salad."

He scoffed. "I'm not eating that."

"Then why ask?"

Morgan ran the yellow light at Riverside. "Let's go to Richard's on Third." He pronounced it *Reeshard's* as if it were a fancy French restaurant.

"Reeshard's? Is that new?"

"You've been."

"I have?"

"Oh, yeah."

"To Reeshard's on Third?" Her face pinched in realization. "Oh, my God. Are you serious? Not Dick's."

He smiled. "What's wrong with Dick's?"

"It's not healthy."

"I'm in the mood for a burger."

"Then let's go to the Onion. You can turn here." She pointed at Sprague Avenue.

"The Onion's not fast," he said as he zipped through the intersection.

"But I can get a salad."

"You're CTF, girlie. You're a meat-eater."

She grabbed the safety bar above her head. "Being Criminal Task Force means I'm a good detective. It doesn't mean I have to eat the crap you do. Slow down."

He ran another yellow at the First Avenue intersection and barely avoided clipping the end of a city bus.

"You're driving like a maniac," Senai said. "Is your blood sugar low?"

"It's lunchtime. There'll be a line."

"For those burgers?"

"It's an institution."

Senai sighed. "This is why I outrun you."

"You outrun me because you're younger."

"So, you're saying I outrun you because you're old."

He shot her an angry glance.

"And you eat garbage."

Morgan clucked his tongue. "Whatever. We're still going to Dick's."

"I don't get a say?"

"I'm the senior detective, and this is my car, so no, you don't get a say."

She scrunched her nose.

"Get some fries. They're a vegetable."

"You're going to die of a heart attack."

"Someday," he said. "Probably."

"With a greasy burger stuck in your mouth."

"If I'm lucky."

He honked at a car that took its damn time pulling into the Chevron. When it was clear, he gunned the Dodge's engine, ran a stoplight long after it flicked red, and turned widely onto Third Avenue.

Senai dropped her cell phone as she anxiously grabbed the dash. "Good Lord, Morgan!" she cried. When the Charger slowed to the current traffic flow, she bent to recover her phone.

"It's your legs," he said.

She straightened. "Excuse me?"

Morgan motioned absently toward her. "You. Your legs."

"What are you talking about?"

"They go all the way up to your neck. That's why you outrun me. It's got nothing to do with my age."

"Okay."

"Or what I eat."

"Keep telling yourself that."

Morgan jerked the wheel, and the car bounced into the parking lot of Dick's Hamburgers. The establishment sat in the shadow of the Interstate-90 freeway, and offramps for both east and west traffic merged right next to it.

"Christ," Morgan said as he cruised through the lot. "Look at the line."

"Let's go elsewhere."

He pulled into a spot and parked too close to the dusty pick-up on Senai's side. After removing the ignition key, he said, "I'll be back."

"I'm coming." Her voice strained as she slipped through the tight fit caused by the neighboring vehicle.

"I thought you wanted a salad," Morgan called as the passenger door slammed.

Morgan was almost in line by the time Senai made it out of the car.

There was no indoor dining at Dick's. Everyone had to wait in line to place an order. If a customer was truly hungry, they could purchase a bag of burgers. Some would take their orders to-go. Others could nosh in their cars. A few may choose to eat at the nearby picnic benches.

As the detectives waited in line, Morgan eyed the crowd. He loved this burger joint because every division of society was represented here. Old and young. Poor and rich. Cops and criminals. Dick's Hamburgers was a metaphorical Switzerland, and everyone came to eat in peace.

Seated at one of the picnic tables was Roy Utt. A burger was jammed into his face as he tried suspiciously hard to avoid looking at Morgan. The shirtless junkie looked terrible. His usually pale skin was sunburned and dirty. His red Converse were tattered, and his baggy jeans were greasy. The Chicago Bulls jersey he usually wore was balled on the bench next to him.

It was unfortunate Utt had slid so far into the drug. He'd been useful for a lot of decent intel over the past couple of years. Probably still would be for a bit longer, but if Utt didn't clean himself up soon, the writing was on the walls.

Morgan stared for a few seconds more until the junkie looked the opposite way.

"Next!" the woman behind the counter hollered.

"That was faster than I expected," Senai said.

Morgan was about to step up to order when he noticed a long-haired white male hurriedly walking away from the burger joint. He wore a black T-shirt and blue jeans. In his hands, he clutched a bag of hamburgers to his chest. The two men made brief eye contact then the guy crouched and sprinted.

"The fuck?" Morgan muttered.

Senai looked over her shoulder. "Who is that?"

"Never seen him before."

The man raced along Third Avenue, crossed at the Frankie Doodles restaurant, then continued northbound on Pine Street. Morgan saw Roy Utt also watching the man who sprinted away. The junkie gleefully ate his burger as if the whole thing were some movie.

"Next," the woman behind the counter said again.

"You want to go after him?" Senai asked.

"No."

The two detectives placed their orders then. Morgan ordered two Whammys and a Coke, while Senai ordered a large fry and a vanilla shake. They stepped back and waited with a group of other customers.

Over at the picnic table, Roy Utt stood and tossed his

trash into a nearby can.

"Wait for the food," Morgan said and began walking away.

"Where are you going?"

"To see an old friend."

Utt grabbed his Bulls jersey and headed for the road.

"Roy!" Morgan hollered as he followed along.

The junkie flinched yet didn't look back. He continued toward the road.

"Come here," the detective shouted over the Third Avenue traffic.

Utt turned around but now walked backward along the sidewalk. "Why?"

"I said so."

"Yo, I didn't do nothin'."

Morgan stopped walking. "Remember what happened the last time I chased you?"

Utt took two more steps then stopped backpedaling. "Aw, c'mon, Morgan."

The detective snapped his fingers and pointed at the ground the way an owner might do toward a misbehaving puppy. "Now. I don't have all day."

The junkie lowered his head and shuffled over.

"Who was that?" Morgan asked.

"Who was who?"

"That mope who took off."

"I didn't see any—"

Morgan snatched Utt by the back of the neck and jerked him closer.

"Hey! You're hurting me."

Several years ago, Roy Utt admitted to Morgan that he had a low tolerance for pain. This bit of information suited the detective just fine, and he used it to his advantage whenever necessary.

"Who was that?" he repeated.

The junkie reached for Morgan's hand but stopped short of grabbing the man's wrist. Utt had been down this path before and knew better than to touch the detective.

"Jesus, Morgan, I never seen the guy before. What do you want from me? Let go."

"Describe him."

"Who?"

Morgan squeezed and jerked Utt closer.

"Ow! I don't know. White dude. He was a white dude!"

"What was he wearing?"

"Blue jeans. Black shirt. Right? Wasn't that what he was wearing?"

Cars continued to whiz by on Third Avenue.

"You swear you don't know him?" Another squeeze.

"Oh, my fuck. No! Who was he?"

"What was he carrying?" Morgan asked.

"What was he carrying? Ow! I don't know. A bag of burgers?"

"That's right. Didn't it look like he was protecting it?"

Utt studied the detective's face. "Now that you mention it."

"Have you ever protected your burgers like that?"

"No. Never."

Morgan released him. "There you go."

The junkie's brow furrowed. "Huh?"

"I want that bag."

"But I don't know him."

"How's that my problem?"

Utt glanced around. "Am I being punked?"

Morgan reached for him again, but the junkie quickly stepped back.

"All right, all right, Morgan! Jesus. The bag. You

want the bag. What do I get out of it?"

"I won't arrest you for the dope in your pants."

Utt looked down at his shoes. "I don't have any dope."

"Empty your pockets."

"Why do I have to do that? You don't have probable cause—"

Morgan snatched him by the neck and yanked him close again. "You stink, Roy. Anybody tell you that?"

Utt raised his hands. "Okay, the bag. I understand."

"Empty your pockets."

"I'll get you the bag!"

The detective released him, but Utt looked dejected. Morgan knew how far he could push and pull a junkie like Utt. He had just threatened him with a stick. That would only get so much love. What he needed to do was offer the man a carrot—something he could really use. "I'll make you a deal, Roy."

Utt looked up expectantly. "What's that?"

"Bring me the bag, and you'll earn a Get Out of Jail Free card."

"For real?"

"You know me. Do I lie?"

"No, man, you don't." Utt looked away briefly. "So, just the bag?"

"Don't be an ass."

"Right. You want what was inside. What if it was just burgers and stuff?"

Morgan smirked. "Really? Do you want the pass or not?"

"Yeah, yeah, for sure, but do I need to bring you the bag?"

"I thought we just clarified that."

Utt shuffled now as if he were growing excited. "What I'm saying is this," he tapped his chest, "do I need to bring you the bag? As in me."

"What are you thinking?"

"Well, what if I get someone else to bring you the bag?"

"You think you can sweet talk that mope into bringing me the bag?"

"If I can find him, maybe."

"Yeah. Fine. He brings me the bag, and you still earn the Get Out of Jail Free card."

Utt licked his lips then rubbed a hand over his face. "Okay. Now, we're talking. What if I get more than one bag?"

"What is this? *Let's Make a Deal*?"

"I'm serious, Morgan. Hear me out. What if I get more than one?"

"He only had one bag, Roy."

"But what if he had two?" Utt's eyes went up as he thought. "Or what if someone else had a bag that has something in it?"

"I guess that depends on what's in the bag."

"Can I get two Get Out of Jail Free cards?" He held up as many fingers. "Or more?"

"We can work something out, Roy."

"What if somebody brings something good? Can they get one of those cards, too? No questions asked?"

This had quickly developed into something Morgan hadn't planned. He couldn't offer amnesty for just anyone. A low-level player like Roy Utt could fall below the radar and be taken care of, but a whole mess of junkies and thieves? That would be hard to do, but the reality that this would be anything more than a giant circle jerk was slim.

Morgan believed Roy Utt could scare up one bag of something—even if he had to steal it—to earn that Get

Out of Jail Free card.

Two bags? Unlikely.

Might Roy convince someone else to jump into this junkie pyramid scheme? Doubtful.

"Yeah, okay," Morgan said. "You got a deal."

Utt tapped his naked wrist. "How much time have I got?"

Morgan considered the question. "It's noon now. Let's say midnight tomorrow. Thirty-six hours."

A grin spread across Utt's face as he backpedaled. "You've never lied to me, Morgan. I'm holding you to this."

"Word is bond, Roy, but you gotta be back here by midnight tomorrow, or the deal is off."

The junkie clapped his hands twice even though he was still holding the jersey. Then he sprinted in the direction the unknown man had run earlier. Utt's sunburnt back disappeared around the corner of Pine Street.

"Midnight!" Morgan hollered.

Nayla Senai walked over with her hands full of food and drinks.

"Was that Roy Utt?" she asked.

Morgan took his bag and soda from her. "Yep."

"Where's he going in such a hurry?"

"To help us make our numbers."

"How's he going to do that?" Nayla asked.

"He's going to get every scumbag in town to bring us a present."

She raised an eyebrow. "Yeah? And what's that?"

"A bag of Dick's."

Senai cocked her head.

Morgan grinned. "I told you I would think of something."

The Legend of Roy Utt

Roy Utt sprinted away from Dick's Hamburgers. His red Converse High Tops loudly slapped the sidewalk, and his right hand clutched a balled-up Chicago Bulls jersey. With this sudden burst of motion, his jeans slipped from his waist.

He had lost more weight recently. Roy had no idea how much as he didn't have access to a scale, and he rarely noticed these types of changes until they became inconvenient. With his free hand, he tugged the jeans back into place. This caused him to hop then waddle before he ran again. The process repeated itself every few strides—hop, waddle, run.

Vehicular traffic zipped along Third Avenue. A diesel truck with a low backend and a rattling engine chugged by. It spewed out a line of thick, dark exhaust.

Unaccustomed to sudden bouts of physical exertion, Roy sucked air through his mouth. The cloying fumes from the truck mixed with the day's stifling heat to create a nauseating blend. His lungs burned. Roy coughed but didn't stop running. He couldn't.

He glanced over his shoulder, noticed a break in the line of cars, and entered Third Avenue at Pine Street. Roy ran, hopped, then waddled before repeating the process.

The lace on his right shoe came undone and swung wildly with each step. Even without Detective James Morgan pursuing him, Roy continued this shuffling pace. He had to—there was a prize to be gained. This out-of-nowhere offer from the cop could change his life. Hell, it might even make him a legend on the streets.

Pain stabbed him in the ribs, and Roy jerked upright. He released his jeans, then skipped and limped for a few steps until he slowed to a walk. Roy sucked for air and pressed a hand against his right side. He rarely ran, and when he did, it was usually with someone chasing him. Morgan and his team had pursued him a bunch of times over the years. Roy could usually fight through aches at those moments because not running meant more pain awaited. Why run now when it wasn't necessary?

Pain for pain's sake was for the freaks.

At the corner of Second and Pine, an older man stood with his arm wrapped around the signpost. Preacher wore slacks and a dirty suit jacket with no shirt. His feet were as filthy and as bare as his chest. His eyes snapped open, and he pointed at Roy. "You're going to hell!"

"No shit," Roy said. "You see a guy run by here?"

Preacher clung to the pole as if he were in the middle of a hurricane. The older man's eyes closed again, and he slurred when he spoke. "You're the devil's agent."

Roy wondered if he meant the real devil or Morgan.

Detective Morgan had many labels—an asshole and a thug came immediately to mind—but the man wasn't a liar. The streets knew for sure—Morgan's word was gold. If he made an agreement, it stuck. The detective had just made Roy the greatest offer of all time—a Get Out of Jail Free card.

Roy might have screwed with Preacher on another day, but he didn't have time for such games now. Instead, he had only one thing on his mind—earning that card.

Kitty-corner from where Roy stood was a 7-Eleven. Two guys sat against the back of the building and watched his interaction with Preacher. Even though Second Avenue was only one-way, Roy checked both directions for oncoming traffic—a lesson he remembered his mother teaching him when he was little. As he was about to step into the roadway, the older man grabbed the basketball jersey he still held.

"Gimme that!" Preacher said.

Anger flashed through Roy, but he didn't bother trying to tug the shirt back from the old man. Instead, he slugged Preacher in the eye.

The older man squealed and released his grip from the garment. With one eye shut, Preacher clung to the pole by the crook of his elbow and his legs churned for purchase on the sidewalk. The older man corkscrewed himself around the metal bar and down to the ground.

A car honked several times as it passed by.

Roy leaned over the fallen man. "Don't ever touch me!" He kicked Preacher in the leg for emphasis.

The older man bounced once and clung tighter to the pole with both arms now. Preacher emphatically shook his head. "It hurts you to kick against the cattle prods!"

Roy scrunched his face. "The hell?"

"Acts," Preacher muttered.

"What?"

The old man's eyes pinched closed and he screamed, "Saul!"

Roy kicked Preacher once more, but this time it was for being a drunk, old zealot.

He looked back toward the 7-Eleven and saw the two men watching him. Roy raised a hand in familiar greeting and stepped into the street.

A Ford F-150 slammed its brakes and honked loudly—one long blare to signal the world at just how careless Roy had been and how self-important its driver was. Roy jumped back onto the sidewalk and lifted a hand in apology.

Behind the wheel, a heavy-set man in sunglasses

yelled through the open driver's window, "Pay attention, you junkie!"

The two men were less than five feet apart. Roy decreased the distance even further by extending his middle finger. "Pay attention to this, you fat bastard!"

The driver's eyes widened, and he frantically yanked at his door handle.

Roy spun around and darted back up Pine Street and into the alley.

***

"Explain it again," Joe said. He ran his fingers through his thick, dark hair. He wore a faded Britney Spears T-shirt torn at the neck, black jeans with holes in the knees, and dirty Reeboks. "I'm having trouble following this."

Roy nodded. "You know Morgan?"

"Who doesn't?"

"He wants a bag—"

"But doesn't care about the dude carrying it?"

"I don't think so."

Joe leaned against the rear of the 7-Eleven and eyed his friend, Tom. "Does that sound like Morgan to you?"

Tom didn't answer but instead sipped from a large cup of soda. The lid of the drink sat on the far side of him. He had remained silent during most of Roy's initial telling while Joe interrupted with mostly inane questions. Roy had partied many times with both men and knew Tom usually kept his thoughts to himself, which probably wasn't difficult with Joe around.

So far, Roy's story had stuttered along, but he knew the situation could devolve quicker with these two. He just needed to know if they saw the guy from Dick's and which way he ran.

The building shaded the three men from the afternoon sun. A patrol car raced by on Second with its lights activated. Its siren, however, remained silent.

Joe watched it until it was out of sight. "Wee-wee-wee, all the way home." He faced Tom. "What? That was funny."

Tom shrugged. His brown hair was tucked behind his ears, and he wore a pair of sunglasses with one arm broken off. His Levi's were faded and torn at the heels, and mud covered his running shoes. Tom's white T-shirt was inside-out to hide whatever logo was on the front.

Joe dismissed his friend's lack of humor with a cluck of his tongue and turned back to Roy. "What's in the bag?"

"He told you," Tom wearily said. "Morgan didn't know."

"I wasn't asking what Morgan knew," Joe snapped. "I was asking about him." He pointed to Roy. "What's in the bag?"

Roy shook his head. "I saw the guy running. That's all."

"Uh-huh." Joe smirked. "I bet you told Morgan you never saw ol' boy before."

"That's right," Roy said. "Never." He glanced between the two friends. "So, did you guys see him run by or not?"

Joe tugged an unfiltered Camel from a crumpled pack, then lit it with a match. He blew out a line of smoke.

Tom slipped the broken sunglasses from his face and studied Roy with an unsettling intensity. Even when Tom was high, he had that same look. It was the type of expressions the cops had, and it unnerved Roy.

He broke Tom's gaze and motioned toward Joe's cigarettes. "Can I have one of those?"

"Not unless you're holding."

Roy was, but he couldn't share. There was only enough for him. If he shared, he'd only get partially well. Then the sickness would overwhelm him by the morning. He had planned to work on that problem today, but this new opportunity took priority. Nothing like this had ever happened to him—Roy had hit the Lotto and gotten Super Bowl tickets in the same day.

Joe offered the pack of cigarettes to Tom by smacking it against his friend's shoulder. Tom accepted them without looking.

"C'mon," Roy said. "Just one. I'm offering you guys something here."

Joe snatched the cigarette from his mouth. "What are you offering? Nothing. You come over here, screwing up our day because you want to know if we saw some jerk-off with a bag. How is that offering us anything? That's you taking. When you find the guy, you score the Monopoly card."

"Get Out of Jail Free," Tom said.

Joe rolled his eyes and turned to his friend in an exaggeratedly dramatic fashion. "May I continue?"

Tom extended his hand. "I'm not stopping you."

"That's exactly what you're doing."

"How'm I doing that?"

"By doing what you're doing. If you're so eager to talk, why don't you go ahead and finally do it?"

"Fine."

"Fine," Joe said.

Tom shook his head then lit his cigarette. As he waved out the burning match, he asked Roy, "How's any of this help us?"

Roy faced Tom now. Maybe he would finally get the whole situation explained. "Morgan wants a bag. Doesn't matter who brings it. Doesn't matter what's inside. As long as there's value to him and it gets to him by tomorrow midnight at Dick's."

"Horseshit," Joe said. He stuck his cigarette between his lips. It bounced as he spoke. "Utter horseshit."

Tom lifted a hand to quiet his friend. "So, as I understand this—"

Joe interrupted. "You're buying this?"

"Hold on. I got another question."

"Now, you're fulla questions?" Joe waved his hands around. "Oh well, please, by all means, continue on, Counselor."

Tom waited for Joe to settle down before focusing back on Roy. "Just so I get this straight, Morgan is offering amnesty to anyone that brings him a bag?"

"From Dick's. That's right."

Joe contemptuously eyed his friend. "The fuck is with you?"

"What?"

"Amnesty?"

"It's a word."

"I know it's a word." Joe swung his hand again. "Look around. This look like a campus to you?"

Roy motioned toward the cigarettes again. "You sure I can't have one?"

"No," Joe and Tom said together.

"Can't you see the big picture?" Tom asked his friend. "Roy's got a deal, and he's cutting us in."

Joe thrust his hand out, and Tom put the cup of soda in it. After taking a healthy drink, Joe wiped his mouth with the back of his hand. "Morgan's full of shit. Roy, too."

"Maybe not," Tom said.

Roy craned his neck to get their attention. "It's for real. I swear."

"It's Willy Wonka," Joe said. "One golden ticket. Everyone is going to be chasing this guy in hopes of getting that bag. The chances of us getting it are ridiculously slim. Why would we even want to try?"

Tom eyed his friend. "Willy Wonka gave away five tickets."

Joe inhaled on his cigarette and held the smoke for a moment. "Right. Five tickets. I forgot." He knocked some ash free from his cigarette. "The blueberry chick and the TV kid are the only ones I remember."

"Mike Teavee," Tom said. "He got sucked into that old television set."

"So cool." Joe tapped his cigarette again. "Who were the others? You recall?"

Roy stepped forward. "So, have you seen the guy or not?" He looked up and down Pine Street. "He came running this way."

Tom's face turned toward the sky, and he dragged on his Camel. "The fat kid."

"Yeah," Joe said. "The fat kid. That's right. What was his name? Goofus Gump or something like that."

"August Goop."

"Are you sure?"

Tom shrugged.

Joe held out his hand and extended three fingers. "Five tickets. Who are the other two?"

Roy waved a hand to get their attention. "Hey? The guy with the bag. Did you see him?"

Tom squinted and looked toward the sky. "Goop, Teavee, and blueberry chick. Wasn't there a second girl?"

"This is going to bug me," Joe said.

Now, Roy waved the basketball jersey like a matador. "The guy with the bag? Did he come by or not?"

Tom absently pointed further down Pine Street, but his

face remained upward.

"He went that way?" Roy asked.

"Veruca Salt," Tom muttered. He looked at his friend with a smile. "That's the other chick."

"Right," Joe slapped his hands together. "Veruca Salt. Awesome work. Hey, did you ever listen to their music? They were fuckin' great. They had that one song."

Tom leaned forward and flicked his cigarette into the street. "I liked Liz Phair better."

"Are you kidding me?" Joe angrily threw the butt of his cigarette to the ground. "The shit you say makes no sense."

Roy gave up waiting. He turned and ran further north.

***

Roy watched her climb out of a BMW without looking back. As soon as she cleared the door, the car drove away. The passenger door slammed closed with the momentum of the sedan.

Liliya Scrimshaw wore powder blue shorts and a black half-shirt. She walked over to the corner of Pacific and Pine, dropped her slouchy purse near her dirty white tennis shoes, then sat on the curb. After digging in the bag, she flipped her long dishwater blond hair back and lit a cigarette. She extended her legs into the street.

As Roy hurried over, she faced him. "Don't even think about it, Roy." She waggled a finger. "Not unless you're paying full price."

"I'm not here for that, Scrimmy."

She appeared hurt. "Why the hell not? Something wrong with me? I don't look good?"

"No," Roy said. "I'm after something hot."

"Hotter than me?" Scrimmy waved her hand along the

side of her pale, bruised legs. "You know you want a taste, Roy. How much you got on you?"

"Not enough."

"You let me decide that. You holding?"

"No," he lied.

"Uh-huh." Her eyes narrowed, and she inhaled on her cigarette. When she spoke next, entrails of smoke drifted from her mouth. "You're looking a little tight."

Roy *was* feeling bad. Hell, that wasn't true. He always felt bad, but he was starting to feel worse. Maybe it was the heat and the running and the burger in his gut. Roy held out his hand for her cigarette. She gave it to him, and he inhaled deeply.

"You sure you're okay, Roy?"

He handed the cigarette back. "I'm fine."

"Yeah, you are." She said it without enthusiasm. Scrimmy smiled now and revealed the brown tooth in the front of her mouth. "Let's deal, Roy. I know you got something in your pocket."

He remembered this game with Scrimmy. Only one time had she given him a break, and that was for a handy in a gas station restroom. The other two times, she completely wiped him out, and those had both been for standing quickies in an alley. Roy wasn't going to say those trades weren't worth the money or drugs he gave up, but he didn't have the time today. "Did you see a guy come running by with a bag of burgers?"

She frowned. "I must've missed him. I've had my head down, you know. Work and all."

Roy glanced around. The more time went by, the less likely he was to find the guy. He'd heard some shit like that said in a movie once. It was about kidnappers or bank robbers—he couldn't remember it clearly.

"Why's this guy so important?" Scrimmy asked.

"It's the bag that's important."

He told her the story then. He didn't leave anything out. At least, he didn't think he did. His stomach was roiling, and he started to feel chilled.

Scrimmy stood and brushed off her butt. "Morgan." The way she said it is the way some people curse.

"It's for real," Roy said.

"I know it's for real." Her gaze drifted up and down Pine Street. "I'm just figuring out how to get in on it."

"You really didn't see the guy?"

Scrimmy shook her head. "I wish I had. Believe that. Now, I gotta find me something to bring Morgan."

Roy smiled. "If you do…"

Her eyes narrowed. "What?"

"I don't know. I was thinking maybe—"

"What were you thinking, Roy? That I'd throw you a freebie?"

He shrugged. "This Morgan thing is legit."

"So?"

"I didn't have to tell you about it."

"I would have heard about it sooner or later."

"No, you wouldn't. This is mine." He tapped his chest. "I made the deal with Morgan. Me."

"Are you strong-arming me, Roy?" Liliya Scrimshaw's face hardened. "Well, this ain't the movies. You pay retail like everyone else." She snatched up her purse and headed east.

"But you gave me a discount once."

She looked back over her shoulder. "That was to get you hooked, you stupid bastard."

***

Roy thought maybe the guy with the Dick's bag had

turned west and headed toward the House of Charity. Lots of guys he knew stayed there. Roy hadn't. Not that it wasn't an option, but if he stayed there, he knew there was no coming back.

His mom had called the place Skid Row while he was growing up. She felt the same way about the Union Gospel Mission, although she seemed to tolerate that one a bit more because they insisted on shoving religious teachings down their visitors' throats.

Roy figured if he never stayed at one of those joints, he still had a chance to clean himself up and get right. He'd lived in some shitty places—the Hope Apartments (before they evicted everyone), an abandoned warehouse on Riverside, a tent encampment down by the river. He couch-surfed all over the city, but there was no way he would ever stay at the House of Charity.

He ran, hopped, and waddled until he made it there.

As he approached the shelter, Maggot Mike hurried over and held up both hands to stop Roy. The two men stood in the middle of Pacific Avenue.

"Is it true?"

Despite the sun blazing down on him, Maggot wore several layers of clothes. Fingerless gloves covered his hands. The man smelled like urine and gasoline—maybe it was just gasoline. Roy couldn't be sure.

"Is it true?" Maggot asked again and tapped Roy's bare chest.

Roy swatted his hand away using the Chicago Bulls jersey. "Is what true?"

"What they're saying." Maggot thumbed toward the street corner where a group of men and women surrounded Joe and Tom. They watched the two men with rapt attention. "They said the cops are giving away Get Out of Jail Free cards."

"Not the cops," Roy said. "Morgan. Detective Morgan."

Maggot's eyes widened with excitement. He lifted his fists in victory and turned around. "It's true!" he shouted. "It's all true!"

The group around Tom and Joe cheered. The two men in the center high fived and laughed with the others.

Roy watched them and grew angry. He needed to go somewhere to think.

***

Elva Lightly plopped a can of beer on the counter and announced the total. As Roy dug into his pocket, he eyed her.

She was in her late sixties with stringy hair that fell to her shoulders. Although her skin was wrinkled and gray, many men who frequented the establishment tried to make time with her. She never flirted with any customers in the bar, however. She'd been in the industry too long to encourage that.

Roy pulled out several crumpled bills and tossed them on the counter. Elva scooped them up deftly then straightened them.

"No tip?"

"I'm tapped out," Roy said.

"Aren't we all," she muttered and wandered off.

After leaving the House of Charity, Roy had wandered over to The Well at the corner of Washington and Second. Roy normally wouldn't spend money to drink in an establishment, but the last thing he needed was to get arrested for public intoxication. Or worse, get rolled for the beer because he wasn't paying attention.

Roy grabbed the can and took a healthy swig. He

didn't want a beer, but what he wanted would put him out of commission for too long. Roy needed to be at his best right now. The prize was too big for him to give in to the chills.

This wasn't pain for pain's sake. This was pain for an ultimate prize. He had to figure out a way to cope with it.

He replayed the image of the crowd cheering around Tom and Joe. He hadn't expected that to happen. Roy thought he might be able to trade that information around town. Get some assistance finding what he needed, maybe help some guys along the way. But those two dirtbags had to go and share the information for free like the streets were some goddamned commune.

Roy angrily swallowed another swig of beer.

Now the information he had was worthless. Well, maybe not worthless, but its value was greatly diminished. If the streets knew Morgan wanted the guy with a bag of burgers, that meant a slew of others might be pursuing him right now. Basically, Roy had nothing to trade anyone.

Since it was unlikely he'd find the guy that ran from Dick's, Roy would need to bring something else to Morgan. What Roy needed was something not many others knew about. Otherwise, that might be in play, too.

All this thinking made Roy's head hurt. His nose ran, and he wiped it with the back of his hand. Now, he was getting the comedown sniffles. Christ.

He lifted the can to his lips and paused.

There was a thing a dead friend of his did. He could give that to Morgan, and no one would get hurt, but it meant going to see his brother-in-law.

***

"Roy Utt," Callum McDougan said. He leaned back in a squeaking office chair and crossed his arms over his barrel chest. "A walking, talking piece of squeeze. You got some pair of balls."

"Nice to see you, too, Callum."

Roy closed the door behind him. They were in the office of McDougan's Tow Yard just off Perry and Second. It had taken Roy more than an hour to walk there after he left The Well. An overhead fan stirred the stale air around. The office smelled of grease and body odor.

"You look like shit."

Roy snuffled, then rubbed a finger under his runny nose.

"Are you using coke now, too?"

"No." Roy sat in one of the pleather chairs in front of the desk. Its seat was ripped in multiple spots. "I got a summer cold, is all."

"Whatever." Callum shifted his weight. "You're not getting any money out of me."

"I don't want any."

"That's like a monkey saying it doesn't want a banana."

"Monkeys don't talk."

Callum's chair fell forward. "You smart-mouthing me?"

Roy diverted his eyes. Callum always made him nervous. "I didn't mean no disrespect."

"Why the hell are you here, Roy?"

"I need to get in the yard." He peered through the window over Callum's shoulder, hoping to see a rusted '64 Chevy Impala SS Coupe. It had been out in the back for years waiting for Callum to start a low-rider project on it, but the man never got around to it. There had been several cars back there waiting for him to begin various plans.

Callum stabbed the desk with a finger. "What makes you think I want you anywhere on my property?"

Roy's gaze returned to Callum. "We're family."

"*Were* family, Roy. I divorced your sister two years ago."

"You did?"

Callum smirked. "Nice of you to notice. I'm sure your sister appreciates the empathy."

Roy looked out the window again. He didn't see the Impala anywhere. Was Callum working on it now? He glanced into the shop, but there were no cars there.

"How come?" Roy asked.

"How come what?"

"How come you and Denise split up?"

"You know why." Callum stood and put his hands flat on his desk. He leaned forward. "You just had to go and open that fat mouth of yours at your mother's funeral."

Roy's attention snapped back to Callum. "I didn't say nothing."

"Bullshit!" The big man slapped the desk. "Denise told me what you said."

"If I said something, I was just spouting off. It didn't mean nothing."

"Spouting off?" Another slap of the desk. "That's what you call it? You tell her about the girls who come through here? After all I did for you?"

Callum abruptly stepped around the large piece of furniture, which caused Roy to jump from his chair.

"Take it easy, Cal." Roy backpedaled and lifted his hands in surrender.

"There's nothing to talk about. You opened your mouth about business you had no business talking about."

Callum continued walking forward until he backed the

smaller Roy against the door.

Roy's hands touched Callum's shoulders. "Hey, man, I'm working on this thing."

"No more of your bullshit, Roy."

"It's not bull—"

Roy never saw the punch that caught him in the belly and doubled him over. Callum stepped back and let him fall to the floor.

"You okay, Roy?"

He coughed and sucked for air. When Roy finally regained his breath, he nodded.

Callum reached down and gently turned Roy's face upward. He looked remorsefully at his former brother-in-law. "Just so you know, Roy, this is me spouting off." He punched Roy across the chin.

***

When Roy awoke, he was still on the floor of the tow office. He slowly pushed himself to his hands and knees. His head hurt, and nausea washed over him.

"Why'd you need in the yard, Roy?" Callum sat nearby in the torn pleather chair.

Roy rolled backward onto his heels which was a bad idea. He touched the floor to stop the room from spinning.

"Well?"

He swallowed the bile that rose in his throat. "The Impala." The words croaked out.

Callum leaned forward and rested his elbows on his knees. "What about it?"

"I came to see it."

A few years back, Roy told a friend about his brother-in-law's tow yard and the cars Callum hadn't gotten around to restoring. The friend climbed the fence one night and hid a gun in the trunk of the Impala. The trunk's lock was broken. Roy got mad at this friend but didn't tell Callum about it. The rules of the street dictated so. When his friend died a couple of days later, Roy quit thinking about the gun and the implications surrounding it.

"What's so important about the Impala, Roy?"

If he could recover the gun from the trunk, he would give it to Morgan. Roy would tell the detective about his dead friend. All that together would likely clear up a couple of murders. Maybe that would be enough juice to earn Roy that Get Out of Jail Free card.

"I like Impalas," Roy said.

"Too bad." Callum sat back into the chair. "It's gone."

"You sold it?"

He nodded. "To some *vato*. He'll trick it out way nicer than I ever would."

Roy tried to stand, but the world still spun. He touched the floor again.

"Lucky I searched the rig before I got rid of it. You wouldn't happen to know anything about what I found, would you?"

Roy shook his head and regretted it immediately. The world hadn't fully stopped spinning yet.

"Uh-huh," Callum said. "You never seemed the type for guns."

"It wasn't mine."

"Serial number was filed off. Looked like an amateur job."

"What'd you do with it?"

"You want to know what I did with that gun?" Callum stood abruptly. "What do you think I did with it? I threw it in the god damned river where it belongs. Someone hides a gun in one of my cars, they're doing it for a reason. Whatever it was, I didn't want it connected to me."

Roy made it to his feet and held onto the wall. "That was probably smart."

"Don't bullshit me, Roy. Why'd you put it there?"

"I told you. It wasn't mine."

"You knew it was there." Callum stepped forward and stuck a finger in Roy's face. "You were coming back for it now."

Roy swallowed and looked away.

"Tell me I'm wrong."

"There's a detective offering a deal—a Get Out of Jail Free card."

Callum shoved Roy. "Get out with that bullshit."

"I'm serious."

"Me, too. Get out!"

Roy put his hand on the doorknob. "I'm sorry to hear about you and Denise."

Callum dismissively flicked his hand. "I don't need your apologies, Roy. I need you to step off. Take your junkie ass and walk out of my life."

***

Roy walked up Perry Street toward Sprague. As he went, he tried to develop a new plan, but nothing came to him. It was still warm out, but he shoved his hands into his pockets. The chills were coming now with a vengeance. He just needed to suffer through them. A couple more hours, and he'd reward himself for his self-control.

Pain for pain's sake was for the freaks. What he was doing was for his future. It made him feel like a citizen.

When he neared the corner of Perry and Sprague, Skeeze the Breeze noticed him.

"Yo!" Skeeze hollered then looked about as if he were afraid he called attention to himself. The man ducked and hurried forward. Whatever he carried in his arms was held like a football—a hand above and one below. When Skeeze neared, he relaxed. It was then Roy noticed Skeeze clutched a bag from Zip's Drive-In.

"I can't believe I found you," Skeeze whispered. He glanced around as if searching for cops. "Check it out." Skeeze opened the Zip's bag. Inside was a dirty ski glove and what appeared to be a used condom.

"The hell?"

"I found them in the alley. What do you think?"

"About what?"

Skeeze flashed a skeptical look. "Is this enough?"

"For what?"

"Don't act that way, Roy. Scrimmy told me all about it." Skeeze frantically looked around again. "We're the only ones in the know, right? Help me out. Is this enough?"

Roy peered into the bag once more. "What the hell am I looking at?"

Skeeze slammed the bag closed and clutched it to his chest. "That's your problem, Roy. You don't know when you're staring at a sure thing."

Roy tugged up his jeans. "Whatever."

Skeeze's laugh revealed his blackened teeth. "That's right—whatever." He hurried further south toward the freeway, a running back wading through an invisible army of linebackers.

***

At Sprague and Perry, a lowered Chevy Caprice jerked toward Roy as its tires squealed in protest at the sudden stop. From the passenger seat, a black man pointed at Roy through an open window.

There were three other men in the car—all were members of the Dead Boys. Roy had seen them around town before. He knew not to mess with them, and they had never taken any interest in him.

"Stay there!" the man in the passenger seat ordered.

Roy backpedaled along Sprague. He didn't know why the Dead Boys would want to talk with him, but he didn't see a reason to stick around and find out.

"Don't do it!" the man commanded as four car doors sprung open.

Roy spun and sprinted. His pants immediately fell, but now he was wearing his Bulls jersey, so he used both hands to tug his jeans into place. His legs wildly whipped as he ran toward the clubhouse of the Wasted Souls MC. Outside, two men stood near their chrome motorcycles.

If Roy could make it to the clubhouse, the men chasing him would likely give up. It wasn't like Roy had any particular affinity toward the Wasted Souls, he just knew they didn't parlay with the Dead Boys.

The two men moved away from their bikes and stood on the sidewalk. The younger man had broad shoulders, big arms, and a short haircut. The other had shoulder-length gray hair, a long gray beard, and a beer gut. Both wore leather vests over black T-shirts and jeans.

Roy could hear the four black men gaining on him. Their footfalls and repeated yells to stop told him as much. Pain stabbed him in the ribs, but he couldn't stop running because whatever they wanted was likely to be worse than what lay ahead.

The two bikers spoke to each other just before Roy

made it to them. The younger one grabbed Roy and turned him around. The biker draped an arm around Roy's shoulders as the four black men slowed to a stop at the edge of the clubhouse.

At that moment, Roy felt a mixture of fear and comfort. He didn't know what would occur next, but he knew he wasn't going to be hurt by the Dead Boys. The Wasted Souls, on the other hand, had no idea who he was.

Metal bars covered the windows of the nearby clubhouse. A steel plate reinforced the front door. Someone painted the warning *Abandon Hope All Ye Who Oppose* above the entry.

The passenger from the car held his hands out to the sides to stop his associates from passing. He then nodded in deference. "Booster."

"Tremaine," the older biker said.

Realizing the two men knew each other, Roy panicked and grasped the arm around his shoulders. It cinched tightly around his throat.

A bolt slid noisily back on the nearby door. Five large men clad in leather and denim filed out to stand behind Booster and his broad-shouldered friend.

The older biker asked, "What brings you to my neighborhood?"

Tremaine lifted his hands. "We didn't come for trouble."

Booster chuckled. "That's good because you're outnumbered."

"We came to talk with him." Tremaine pointed at Roy.

"This little maggot?" Booster eyed Roy. "What's your name, boy?"

The arm around Roy's neck tightened further, and he uttered his name.

Booster's attention returned to Tremaine. "What could this little turd possibly have done to get your interest?"

"He made a deal with Morgan."

"That dirty bastard?" The men behind Booster laughed in agreement. "He can choke on it for all we care."

"No disagreement," Tremaine said, "but when the man offers a Get Out of Jail Free card, you listen."

The bikers stopped laughing, and Booster asked. "A what?"

"You heard me right." Tremaine pointed at Roy. "That's what's brought us to your doorstep."

Booster stepped forward so he could see Roy better. "Hey, boy. Is what he says true?"

The arm around Roy's neck cinched so tight he couldn't speak. He anxiously tapped the biker's bicep for relief, but none came. Now, Roy nodded as emphatically as he could. Darkness seemed to be closing in on him.

Booster slapped Roy's head. "How's this pissant know the terms of Morgan's offer?"

Tremaine shrugged. "That's what I want to find out."

The older biker said, "Ease up. Let him spill."

The arm around Roy's neck suddenly relaxed, and he was shoved into the middle of the two groups. He bent over with his hands on his knees, and he greedily sucked for air.

"Let's hear it, boy," Booster said. "Don't hold nothing back. Your good health depends upon it."

Roy's heart raced, and he fought the urge to run into the street—it was the only way for him to flee. They would catch him, he knew. Or worse, he would get hit by a car. The best he could do was tell the truth.

"It's like this," Roy said, and he told them everything.

When he finished, Tremaine eyed Booster. "What do you think?"

The older biker tugged on his beard. "I think Morgan is fishing for idiots."

"Probably going to get a boatload of them, too."

Booster smirked. "Sneaky sumbitch."

"Seconded." Tremaine rolled his eyes. "He never fails to amaze."

"Like I said, he's a dirty bastard."

Tremaine nodded once more before heading back toward his car. His associates followed.

"Let's go," Booster said and waved his crew inside.

When the door to the clubhouse closed, the lock slid back into place.

Roy Utt was left alone on the sidewalk. The chills were back, and he hugged himself tightly. Tiredness overwhelmed him, which was horrible since he was running out of time to find something for Morgan.

***

Roy awoke with a start. The chills were gone now, and he'd slept for some time. It was dark, and he had no concept of what time it was. He stood and felt the soreness in his bones. The world inside still felt warm, but he knew that wouldn't last now that he was awake and on his feet. It wouldn't be long before the ache for more medicine started. Unfortunately, he used the last of it before he slept.

Somewhere a bird fluttered, and he looked for it. He was inside an abandoned warehouse. Empty racks and broken pallets were everywhere. He remembered now. He broke in to find a safe place to use.

Roy coughed and tried to shake the cobwebs from his head. He needed to get his priorities set. They were simple.

Get medicine.

Get money for medicine.

Get food.

Roy started for the exit and stopped. He turned around, trying to remember where he came in. He blinked and rubbed his eyes. Where the hell was the exit?

When he finally found his entry point—a kicked-in door at the rear of the building—he walked out. He stumbled into the alley and shielded his eyes against the bright sunlight.

On the sidewalk now, he shuffled toward downtown with his head lowered. The overhead sun seemed especially ruthless, as if it were attempting to be cruel just to him.

Up ahead, a patrol car sat curbside. A woman Roy knew as Barley stood with a female cop. Barley wore a dirty yellow dress over gray sweats and combat boots. Her Los Angeles Dodgers baseball hat was turned backward, and she rubbed her hands excitedly together.

As Roy approached, the two women seemed to be talking in a relaxed conversation.

The officer peered into a bag from D'Lish's Hamburgers. "What the hell is this?"

"It's a knife," Barley said.

"Is that blood?"

Barley nodded. "My boyfriend's."

The cop quickly turned her body, so her gun side was away from Barley.

Roy stopped and stared at the bag the officer held. Memories flooded back to him. He'd forgotten what he was supposed to be doing. The sickness had overtaken him before he used his medicine. It was only supposed to be a short break. Maybe it was. It was still light out after all, but it seemed brighter than he remembered.

"What day is it?" he asked.

The cop pointed at Roy. "Stay back."

Roy lifted his hands. "What day—"

"Stay back!"

Barley smiled at him. "Hey, Roy. Have you gotten your card yet?"

The cop activated her shoulder mike. After announcing her call sign, she said, "Start another unit."

"What day is it?" Roy asked Barley.

"It's today," she said with a smile. "It's beautiful, isn't it?"

The officer pointed at Barley. "Step back."

Barley shuffled backward as she continued to rub her hands. "So, how do we go about it?"

"About what?" the cop asked.

"The Get Out of Jail Free card?"

The cop seemed genuinely surprised by her question. "You stabbed your boyfriend."

Barley smiled. "Yeah, but it's okay. I'm getting a Get Out of Jail Free card for it." She faced Roy. "Tell her it's okay."

The cop eyed him.

"What day is it?" he asked.

"Stay back," she ordered.

"Just tell me what day it is."

"Saturday." The cop pointed at him. "Now, get back."

Roy didn't hesitate. He ran across the street, holding his jeans as he went.

"Tell her about the card!" Barley yelled.

***

At the intersection of Browne and Riverside, Roy looked over at a mid-seventies Camaro. The window was down, and the stereo played some annoying classic rock. Behind the steering wheel, a bald man stared straight ahead.

"What time is it?" Roy asked.

The driver pretended not to hear and turned up the radio.

"Hey!" Roy shouted. "What time is it?"

Looking at him now, the driver sneered. "Who do I look like? Big fucking Ben? Get a watch."

The Camaro accelerated through the intersection.

Roy threw his arms into the air.

A Toyota RAV4 pulled up next to him, and an elderly woman stuck out her hand. Between two fingers was a twenty-dollar bill. "Get something to eat."

Roy grabbed the money. "Thank you," he said. As he stepped away from her vehicle, he asked, "Do you know the time?"

The woman glanced at her dashboard. "It's almost noon." A horn blared behind her, and she accelerated away.

Twelve hours, Roy thought. He was down to twelve hours and no closer to having anything to deliver to Detective Morgan.

But he now had twenty bucks.

***

Elva Lightly slid a beer in front of Roy. "This one's on the house." Her hand remained wrapped around the can, however, so Roy refrained from touching it. The fact that Elva continued to smile at Roy made him uncomfortable. He'd never heard of anyone ever getting a free beer from the Well.

"There's talk you got yourself a Get Out of Jail Free

card."

Roy glanced around at the others sitting in the low light of the bar. Three men studied him with practiced hunger—the type learned by years of hard living.

"Is that true?" Elva asked.

He turned back to her. "Mostly."

Elva pulled the beer away. "The hell does that mean?"

"I'm working on it."

"Is this one of your scams?"

Roy checked out the others again before facing Elva. "It means I've got to bring something to a detective. When I do, he'll reward me."

"For being a rat?"

"That's not what this is about."

Elva reluctantly let go of the can and stepped back. Unenthusiastically, she said, "Drink up."

Roy grabbed the beer and drank ravenously.

"What are you going to do with it?"

He wiped his mouth with the palm of his hand. "Save it 'til I need it, I guess."

"Like a rainy-day fund?"

Roy shrugged, then took another healthy swallow.

"Want to trade for it?"

He lowered the can. He hadn't thought about it. Roy wondered what he might be able to get for a card like that. He looked at the others again. The three men whispered amongst themselves now. "What are you thinking?"

"I don't know," Elva said. "Guess that depends on the legitimacy of the card."

"Ever deal with a detective named Morgan?"

Elva frowned. "He's behind this?"

"You don't think it's good?" Booster's words echoed in Roy's ears.

"I've been around long enough to know two things." Elva looked at the others in the bar and shook her head. A collective moan came from the low light. "If Morgan said it, it's true. He'll hold to his word. That's the type of man he is."

"Then what's the problem?"

Elva leaned an elbow on the bar. "Be careful what you wish for. Morgan will give you exactly what you want. Only it won't be what you wanted."

Roy cocked his head. He had never known Elva to speak in riddles before. "I don't understand."

"And you won't until it's too late. That's how it works with Morgan. Take some advice—sometimes the best deal is the one you don't do. Walk away from this one."

***

Roy walked along First Avenue. The afternoon sun warmed his skin, but it couldn't stop the shakes. He didn't have time to stop and score. Since he only had a few bucks, he would have to pull a quick job, and his brain was clogged with getting Morgan what he needed. Coming up with a creative way to raise some bread didn't seem possible right now.

Maybe he could borrow the medicine, although that seemed unlikely. Dealers didn't extend credit, and he didn't have any friends who'd lend the amount he needed to get straight—he'd worn out any goodwill with them.

What if he did manage to get his hands on some? He couldn't risk using any and crashing out beyond midnight. He needed what little remained of his wits. Even now, his thoughts seemed murky.

Roy sat on the parking lot wall at the corner of Howard and First to further ponder his predicament.

A city bus drove by, and Roy lowered his head to avoid the exhaust fumes.

Maybe he should just pull a job. Go in and burglarize an office somewhere. He looked up. Men and women in business suits walked by him as if he didn't exist. He couldn't break into an office now. It was still too early. He'd have to wait until at least six. It was stupid to think otherwise.

The pain in his gut was real, though. He didn't need to put up with this. Pain for pain's sake was for the freaks.

"The future is now," he muttered to himself. His sister had that poster on her wall when they were kids.

Shit, he thought. Denise was divorced. He should go see her. Maybe she would give him a few bucks to help with the pain.

A patrol car cruised by. Roy lifted his head in time to see the cop. The guy didn't even look his way.

Booster had been right—Morgan was fishing for idiots. Roy shivered and hugged himself. When he turned his face toward the sun, he squinted.

Those guys didn't know Morgan the way Roy knew the detective. Elva Lightly had confirmed what he knew—Morgan was true to his word.

Yet, she had warned him of something. What was it?

Roy lowered his head again and tried to concentrate.

Did Denise still live in the Shadle neighborhood? How long would it take him to walk up there? He did it once a few years ago. It would take two hours, at least. Maybe he could catch a bus, maybe borrow someone's bus pass. Who did he know who had one?

Roy looked up again when he heard voices.

Two men neared him on the sidewalk. Each of them held a white bag—one had the logo of Taco Bell while the other had the symbol for McDonald's. The way they kept the bags—by the bottom as if they were delivering entrées for a fancy restaurant—led Roy to believe they weren't carrying their lunches.

"Hey," he said.

The man with the Taco Bell bag slowed. The other continued walking.

"What've you got in there?" Roy asked.

"Screw," the guy said. "This isn't a charity."

Roy watched them both walk off eastward. Everyone was after that Get Out of Jail Free card, and a pang of jealousy zinged through him. How many would Morgan actually give away?

Elva's admonishment came to him then. She warned Morgan's delivery of the promise might not be exactly what he expected.

But Morgan would deliver on the promise.

Roy remembered playing Monopoly as a kid. Get Out of Jail Free was written right on the card. It didn't get any simpler than that.

He abruptly stood. The shakes were gone. Roy Utt was back on the mission.

***

"What time is it?" Roy asked.

"Time for you to get a watch," Decker said.

"I'm serious."

Pete Decker was a do-gooder—one of the many citizens who volunteered their time around downtown to help folks on hard times. Decker hadn't always been a citizen, though. The green slacks and black T-shirt didn't hide the tattoos running down his arms or those peeking above his neckline. Many had been drawn while in prison. Decker was a man who walked through the shadow of death but was now treading the path of light.

The two men stood in the mouth of an alley near Jefferson and Second. Roy had run aimlessly about for the past several hours. He tried unsuccessfully to come up with an idea. Everything he envisioned fizzled under the harsh light of reality, but he watched others scamper by clutching burger bags in their hands. How could those animals come up with a plan when he couldn't?

Roy *had* had a plan, he reminded himself. A good one, too, but Callum threw the pistol away. He probably did it on purpose to get back at Roy. If Roy didn't get Morgan's prize, it would be Callum's fault. Denise was smart to divorce him.

Pete Decker's eyes narrowed as he fingered the silver cross around his neck. "This about the bag?"

"You heard?"

"Word travels fast."

Roy nodded.

Decker pursed his lips then made an exaggerated gesture to check the silver watch around his wrist. "Six-fifteen."

"Jesus," Roy said, "I'm running out of time."

"He's not going to help you."

"Who?"

"Jesus." Decker shook his head. "You're using the Lord's name in vain."

Roy's face pinched. "Are you going to help me or not?"

"Say you're sorry."

"For what?"

Decker cocked his head.

He rolled his eyes. "I'm sorry for using the Lord's name."

"Not to me, dumb ass." Decker pointed into the sky.

"Say it to him."

Roy's shoulders slumped. "For real?"

Decker crossed his thick arms.

Clasping his hands, Roy looked skyward. "I'm sorry for using your name in vain."

"Amen," Decker said.

"Amen. Now, will you help me?"

Decker leaned against the building and rubbed the cross between his thumb and forefinger. "I got nothing."

"Jesus."

***

The sun was down, but it was still warm out.

Roy walked along Main Avenue past River Park Square. The clock outside the mall showed it to be after ten.

Less than two hours until Morgan's deadline.

He would have liked to imagine he was out of options, but he never had any to begin with. Had Morgan known this all along? Did he send Roy on this wild goose chase just to keep him clean for most of the day?

If that was the case, screw him. It was time Roy started thinking about himself.

He needed to score.

Roy was a burglar by trade, but times were desperate. He needed to change his game. Maybe he should find a nice, fat mark and roll them. Take a wallet or a purse and go get some medicine. After that, his problems would just melt away.

He glanced around. There were plenty of sheep waiting to be shorn. Roy slowed. Which were the best? Young ones or old? Old, he decided. They probably had more money, and they wouldn't fight back. A man or a woman? He liked the idea of robbing a man—it seemed like the right thing to do, but an old woman was probably safer.

Roy had stolen from people when they slept, but that was wholly different than knocking over a citizen while they were upright and aware. Not only did it take a particular set of skills, it took guts. A lot more guts than a burglar had.

As Roy walked, he scanned the pedestrians around him for a likely target. He would find one, follow her for a while, then steal her purse. That was his plan.

He saw a woman walking near the Parkade that checked all the boxes. She must have been in her late fifties, maybe early sixties—a nice-looking woman with silverish hair and a summer dress. A heavy purse draped over her shoulder. Her right hand clutched the leather handbag. In her left, she held a large doggy bag— probably from some fancy restaurant.

Roy followed her for a bit until they came to the intersection at Stevens Street and stopped due to the red light. Traffic flowed in front of them.

He stayed a step behind her. His heart raced as he tried desperately to determine a place to do it. When should he grab the purse? He could do it now. He *should* do it now.

Just grab the handbag and run. Maybe head down to Peaceful Valley, find a spot along the river where he could go through it in peace. That seemed like a decent plan. Not perfect, but workable. On the count of three, he decided.

One.

Two.

The woman turned to him, and her gaze quickly took him in.

Roy's excitement switched to fear. She'd seen him

now. She'd be able to describe him to the cops.

Abandon the plan, the rational part of his brain screamed.

Grab the purse, the medicine demanded.

On the count of three, he quickly resolved once more.

One.

Two.

"Are you hungry?" the woman asked. "I ordered some pan-roasted chicken but hardly touched it." She extended the large white bag.

Dumbly, Roy accepted her offer with both hands. He stared at the large white bag like all his problems had just been solved.

"Have a nice night." The woman crossed the street.

Two hours, Roy thought. There were less than two hours left, and the answer had finally come to him.

***

Roy Utt sat cross-legged at the corner of Stevens Street and First Avenue. He continually watched for anyone passing by. The traffic was considerably thinner here than it was down by the mall, but Roy knew he had a better chance of success in this neighborhood.

Fishermen go where the fish are biting.

Morgan is fishing for idiots, Booster had said. Roy was doing the same now.

While he waited, Roy ate pan-roasted chicken with his fingers. A Styrofoam container lay open on his lap. The large white paper bag had blown away several minutes ago. He didn't see what the big deal was about this bird. Roy preferred the chicken sandwich from McDonald's. That's the problem with rich people, he thought. Always paying too much for items that aren't as good.

When Roy finished the chicken, he dipped his fingers into the mashed potatoes. They were too creamy for his liking. He preferred them lumpy, the way they came out when made from the box. This overly smooth texture didn't stop him from eating, though. It was the first food he'd eaten all day.

There were some green and red vegetables in the container, too, but Roy hadn't willingly eaten a vegetable since he was in grade school. He flipped the Styrofoam box to the sidewalk and stood.

This fishing hole sucked, so he moved south.

That's when Roy saw him in the railroad's underpass—Skag. The man slumped against the wall. Clutched in his arms was a small, white bag.

Maybe he was dead, Roy thought. Could he be so lucky?

He glanced around, making sure no one was nearby, then bent over Skag. The man smelled like shit. Had he crapped his pants when he croaked?

Roy gingerly grabbed the bag and pulled. Slowly, it slid from Skag's arms. It almost cleared the man's grasp when Skag's eyes popped open.

The old junkie screamed, "Rape!"

"Guh!" grunted Roy.

Skag clutched the bag to his chest. "Rape!"

Redetermined, Roy reached for the paper bag. "Give it to me."

"Rape!" Skag rolled away, hiding the paper bag underneath him.

"Hey, you!" someone yelled from down the block. "Leave him alone!"

Frightened by the prospect of being arrested for accosting Skag, Roy stood and ran.

"Rape!" Skag yelled again.

***

Reality finally hit home as Roy walked west along Second Avenue—he couldn't do it. Opportunity had knocked, but he was unable to open the door. His stomach roiled, and he sniffled. The shakes were back, too. He'd gone the whole day without using and this was his reward—a night spent without. He would have to score quickly, or life would get miserable fast. Hell, it was already miserable. Who was he kidding?

Roy was almost to Post Street when he noticed a crumpled white paper bag in the parking lot of a gas station. He picked it up and smoothed it out. It looked like a bag from Dick's. Maybe it wasn't, but it could be, and that's all that mattered. An idea formed as he wiped his nose with the palm of his hand.

Perhaps he didn't need to give Morgan something real. If the detective thought it was real enough to work as a case, then maybe he'd dole out the card. Yeah, Roy thought with a sense of satisfaction, this was an idea that could work.

He didn't know what time it was, but it had to be near midnight. Time was short, so he had to hurry. Roy headed back toward Dick's. As he went, he kept his eyes on the ground. He quickly found a hypodermic needle and dropped it in the bag.

Someone overdosed with it, he imagined. No, Roy corrected himself. Someone was poisoned. That would be the story since poisons were so much more interesting.

He walked faster and scanned the ground. Roy soon found a rock that appeared to have something on it. He lifted it into the night sky. Blood, he decided and plopped it into the bag. Someone was poisoned then clubbed with the rock. He liked where the story was heading.

Roy tugged up his jeans and hurried again.

When he passed The Well, Roy found a parking stub for a nearby lot. He put that into the bag, too. Roy wasn't sure how that would fit into his story, but—

A witness, he quickly decided. Crimes get solved with witnesses. That's usually how Roy got himself into trouble. Someone saw the victim get poisoned then clubbed over the head.

"Good," Roy muttered.

The door to The Well opened, but he didn't bother to look back. Roy pushed forward and was picking up speed now.

Time was short, so he decided other items for the bag probably weren't necessary. He had two murder weapons and a possible witness. That should be enough to get Morgan digging into a case. Enough for the detective to cough up a Get Out of Jail Free card.

Roy hopped once as he was about ready to run. Then he saw it—a leather glove. He stopped immediately, snatched it up, then shoved it into the bag. The story would be perfect now. Morgan had to believe it—two murder weapons, a glove, and a possible witness. All Roy had to do was get it to the detective then spin the story.

Roy could do that. He had to do it. There was no other choice.

"What's in the bag?"

He turned to see three men. Roy recognized them immediately from The Well. Had they been drinking there all afternoon?

"Give us the bag," one of them slurred.

"The fucking bag," another demanded. "Now!"

Roy didn't wait for the third one to offer his thoughts. He simply ran. As Roy did, his pants slipped below his waist. He jerked them back into place with his free hand. His sprint now became a leaping waddle.

Heavy footfalls fell behind him. The men demanded he "Stop," "Come back," and "Knock it the fuck off," but Roy refused to do any of that.

Pain stabbed him in the side, but he didn't pull up. He couldn't. Stopping now meant getting beaten by the three men and losing the Get Out of Jail Free card. He was too close to lose it all.

The footsteps fell away behind him, and Roy continued to run. The pain became worse, and nausea arose. He bent and vomited but continued shuffling forward. Roy glanced over his shoulder to see the three men still there. They were slower than before, but they hadn't stopped either.

Roy ran through the intersection at Browne, narrowly avoiding a car. He leaned forward and pressed his elbow against his side. His fingers dug into his jeans to hold them up. His right hand clutched the bag of contrived evidence to his chest.

He crossed the street and entered a church's parking lot, cutting diagonally through the block.

Roy sucked desperately for air, wheezing loudly as he ran. The pain in his side, the burning in his lungs, and the heaviness of his legs all made him feel like he was going to die.

He screamed against the discomfort. It couldn't beat him. Not now. Not when he was so close to the end.

Division Street lay ahead. When he burst from the alley, Roy turned right. Dick's Hamburgers was directly ahead. The large multicolored pylon sign was turned off. The restaurant had closed for the night, but the parking lot remained full.

Roy looked over his shoulder again. The three men

were even further back. He hadn't lost them, but if he could make it to Dick's, Morgan would be there. His safety would be assured.

A Dodge Charger—Morgan's—sat near the front of the lot. This swelled Roy's heart with hope, and he felt a resurgence of energy. That quickly faded when he noticed most of the other vehicles were patrol cars.

A crowd gathered in the lot, and they appeared to be celebrating something. Detective Morgan stepped out of the mass of people and moved toward the edge of the lot.

"Roy!" he hollered. He tapped his watch. "You got three minutes. Pick up the pace."

A group of police officers moved behind the detective and cheered.

"Let's go, Roy!" someone yelled.

"Hustle, man, hustle!" shouted another.

Roy didn't know why the cops were rooting for him, but he leaned forward and propelled himself faster. The pain in his side worsened like a knife twisting between his ribs.

He couldn't stop. Wouldn't stop.

Morgan swung his arm like a third base coach sending a runner home. "Don't quit now, Roy! You've almost made it!"

Roy stumbled but kept moving. He clutched his pants and the bag to his waist. When he crossed into the parking lot, the group of cops applauded him. No one had ever cheered for Roy Utt, and it felt like he'd just hit the game-winning basket for his high school's team.

He bent at the waist and smiled at all the cops. Several of them came over and patted him on the back. They said things like, "Nice work," "Way to go," and "Good hustle."

Even Morgan rested a hand on Roy's shoulder. "You

showed me something, kid. I didn't think you were going to make it." He motioned to his partner, the black woman. "Senai said you wouldn't come through."

She held open her palms in a what-can-I-say manner. "I apologize, Roy. You did good."

Morgan's grin was discomforting. He put his arm around Roy's shoulder and stood him up. "Is that puke on your shirt?" The detective stepped back.

Roy's gaze swept over the patrol cars. It seemed the backseats had occupants in them. His smile faded. "What's going on?" he asked through gasps of air.

"You're a legend, Roy. Tell him he's a legend, Senai."

The female detective shrugged. "You're a legend."

Morgan laughed. "We made so many arrests in the last thirty-six hours we flooded the jail. They were forced to erect an emergency tent to deal with the overload." Morgan shook his head in disbelief. "The sheriff called the chief and blew a gasket about what we were doing. Just beautiful." The detective motioned at the occupants of the patrol cars. "These are just the latest fish we caught."

Booster's words came back to him then. *Morgan is fishing for idiots.*

The detective playfully punched Roy in the arm. "You did this, Roy. I still can't get over it."

Several faces pressed against the rear windows of the patrol cars. Angry men and women stared at him.

"I didn't do this," he whispered.

"The hell you didn't. I don't know what you said out there, but you lit a fire under this damn city. So many dirtbags came out from hiding that it was like they were on a sinking ship." Morgan grinned like a kid in a candy store and reached for the bag Roy held. "What'd you bring me?"

Roy tried to get it back, but it was too late. Morgan was already looking inside. The detective's brow furrowed.

"The hell is this?"

"Someone was poisoned," Roy said meekly.

"Who?" Senai asked.

"A guy."

The female detective folded her arms. "A guy?"

"What's with the glove?" Morgan asked. "Is O.J. in town?"

Senai smirked.

"You know what?" Morgan rolled the top of the bag down. "It doesn't matter. This could be full of dog shit, and you would still earn a Get Out of Jail Free card."

One of the uniformed cops yelled, "Deputize him, Morgan!"

The group of officers laughed in support. Several of them clapped.

Across the street, the three men from The Well watched what was occurring. Roy noticed them and immediately looked to those occupants in the rear seats of the patrol cars. "I don't want it," he said.

Morgan glanced at Senai before saying, "But we had a deal, Roy. I've got to hold up my end of the bargain. That's how this word-is-bond thing works."

The faces staring at Roy were too much to take. "Arrest me."

Morgan scrunched his nose. "The hell?"

"Please," Roy said. "I can't walk out of here. Otherwise, everyone will know I'm part of this."

"Part of it?" Morgan swung his hands like a showman at a circus. "You're directly responsible, Roy. Without you, none of this would have happened. I might even ask the mayor to give you a key to the city."

Roy grabbed the detective's jacket. "Don't fuck around, Morgan. Arrest me."

"Let go," Morgan said. The humor faded from his eyes, and his face hardened. "Never put your hands on me."

Several of the uniformed officers drifted closer.

"What if I pushed you?" Roy asked. "Would that do it?"

Morgan looked at the other cops. "I wouldn't advise that, Roy."

Roy angrily shoved Morgan.

The detective took a half-step back but held up his hands to stop the other officers from advancing. "It's okay."

"Take me in," Roy pleaded. He stuck out his hands as if preparing for handcuffs. He showed his wrists to the other officers, but none of them moved. "I assaulted an officer. Why aren't you arresting me? Take me in!"

"They can't do that, Roy." Morgan's eyes narrowed. "You had a Get Out of Jail Free card, but that little stunt just cost you. Now, I've kept my word."

"Yeah," Roy muttered as he glanced around. "You did."

"We're square, Roy."

More uniforms surrounded Morgan.

Roy's gaze swept over the patrol cars again. The faces in the back watched him with eagerness. The three men from The Well eyed him intently. Roy's attention returned to the detective. "I'm really sorry about this, Morgan."

The detective shook his head. "This will end badly for you."

Pain for pain's sake was for the freaks. This was for his future.

Roy slugged Morgan in the gut.

The detective didn't move from either the punch or the desire to hurt Roy. Instead, he stayed still.

Roy's eyes widened in terror as the officers surrounding Detective James Morgan swarmed him. They grabbed Roy and tackled him to the ground. Out of reflex, he fought back. Hands clutched at his wrists, but he yanked free and punched anything that moved.

Several cops yelled, "Stop resisting!"

Knee strikes landed in Roy's midsection as he wriggled and struggled. He quickly lost the will to continue, though, and his arms were yanked behind his back and cuffed.

Morgan squatted next to Roy's head. "You had it made, Roy, but you just couldn't let it be."

Roy grunted under the weight of several officers. "You set me up."

"I was trying to help you out," the detective said, "but you were too dumb to know it." Morgan stood and went over to the garbage can. He tossed Roy's bag of debris into it. "At least, it looks like you didn't work too hard for that sack of crap."

The officers jerked Roy to his feet.

Morgan eyed him one final time. "Take care, Roy." He and Senai walked over to the Dodge Charger, climbed in, and drove away.

An officer tugged on Roy's arm. "Let's go, Legend. Time for booking. I'm sure there's going to be a lot of people who want to say hello to you."

In the Pocket

The businessman strode confidently out of Riverpark Square. He didn't carry any shopping bags, so perhaps he ate lunch at the downtown mall. He pressed a cell phone to his left ear while his right hand gestured wildly. A dark blue suit hung nicely from his broad shoulders, but the swing of its pockets seemed off. The left flopped heavily while the right swayed with the rhythm of his gait. He turned left and headed east along Main Street.

I was stuck at the crosswalk with cars between us. Dodging vehicular traffic while running to catch up to the guy would draw too much attention. I abandoned my plan to cross the street and hurried eastbound on the sidewalk. I walked quickly, almost skipping, to get ahead of my quarry.

A group of attractive women noticed the executive when they walked by, yet he didn't seem to care. He continued to chatter into his phone and gesticulate wildly.

The lunchtime crowd was out to take advantage of the sunny afternoon. The businessman seemed unimpressed by it all. He gestured while he talked and repeatedly pointed at nothing, as if emphasizing something important.

I waited for him at the intersection of Main and Wall. When he got to the corner, he stopped and waited for the light to change. We faced each other, but he had no clue I even existed. He checked his watch and looked both ways, as if he were about to cross against the light. A car was coming, so he remained on his side of the street. Several people stood nearby him and waited for the light to change.

Two men moved next to me. Their conversation sounded something about real estate.

"The closing is set for tomorrow. Can you believe he's doing that deal?"

"How big is the fee? I hear it's six figures."

"That's what I heard, too. The fucker."

The light changed, and everyone entered the crosswalk. I positioned myself in my quarry's path. His focus was somewhere over my shoulder. He continued to gesture with his free hand as he spoke. His tanned face was perfectly shaved, and his hair appeared recently cut.

I stumbled and fell into him.

The executive caught me with his free hand. He spun me around—an impromptu pirouette—but he never stopped talking into the phone. "Let's counter."

"Sorry," I said.

He let go of my waist and nodded. As he backpedaled, he waved once. "Take it up another quarter mil. That's right."

I waved back.

"They'll take it. What other choice have they got?"

He spun and hopped up onto the sidewalk.

***

When I returned to my apartment, I tossed three wallets onto my kitchen table. I grabbed a celebratory Coke from the fridge and cracked it open. I stopped drinking after high school, not because I had a problem with alcohol, but because it was simply too expensive to waste money on. Now, the concept of imbibing seemed strange. Why would I want to dull my senses when I needed them sharp for my chosen profession?

It was time to go through the spoils.

The first wallet was from a woman outside of the Davenport Hotel. She wasn't an intended mark. Instead, I accidentally bumped into her. However, her purse was open, and my hand snaked into it. Out of habit, one might say. We each went on our way after I apologized for the accident.

I'm non-threatening. I do my best not to look like a thief or someone down on their luck. Instead, I try to look like a Wall Street trader. Those guys are the real crooks, and no one even bats an eye when they walk into a room. Even after the market crashed, society idolized the greedy bastards. Hollywood continued to make movies about them. People vote them into office against their own best interests.

It's the disguise those bastards wear that does it—I'm sure of it. It's hard to think of a guy in a suit and tie as a criminal. Think about what our politicians have done to the country, and they get reelected. That's why I wear a suit—I even spent the extra money to tailor it.

My skin tone doesn't hurt. Consider it taking advantage of my privilege. I grew up in the foster care system, so pale skin didn't help me back then. Now, I'll use it to my advantage any way I can. We all do what we must to get by.

The woman's wallet contained one hundred thirty-seven dollars and six credit cards, four of which were department store cards. I expected more cash. The department store cards were garbage; no one except a high school kid would buy them. But the Visa and Mastercard would get a reasonable price. I separated the cash and stacked the two plastic cards.

I sent everything else in the wallet—driver's license, insurance card, department store cards, and AARP membership—through the nearby shredder. The wallet itself would go into the apartment's dumpster later that night.

The second wallet came from a black guy who had wandered out of Chili's. His suit looked tailored, so I targeted him. The guy even said, "Excuse me. My bad," when I bumped into him.

Inside his wallet were five one-hundred-dollar bills, three credit cards, and two tickets to an upcoming Mariners game. I added his plastic to the stack and mixed the five hundred with the other cash. Maybe I could drive to Seattle and pawn the tickets to some unsuspecting sucker. I've never been to an actual game and rarely watched them on TV. The Mariners have never been relevant in my lifetime.

I'd have to check the resale value of the tickets to see if they were worth the time and effort to go over the Cascade Mountains. The problem with scalping the baseball tickets is the actual owner could report them stolen. There was a trail back to me if someone sat in those seats. I flicked the tickets several times before deciding. I dropped them into the shredder.

The rest of the wallet's contents were a mixture of pictures and receipts. It all went into the shredder.

The final wallet came from the businessman who had walked out of the mall. The first two wallets were underwhelming, but this one had the hum of something big. The billfold stood tall and opened like a paperback. I rubbed it between my hands and said, "Come on, baby. Big bucks, no whammies." I'd learn to say that from watching reruns on the Game Show Network.

In the executive's wallet were various bills adding up to one hundred eighty-six dollars. I flayed the cash like the high rollers do in the movies.

"That's it?"

The mystical hum was nothing but hokum. Still, I took the cash and added it to the pile.

The right side of the wallet held five gold and platinum credit cards. I spread them out like a deck of cards. At least there wasn't a department store card in the bunch. I slapped them together and added them to the pile of plastic.

In the left pocket of the wallet was a stack of small photographs. I tugged them out and looked at the top one. A little girl with pigtails, probably seven or eight years old, stared at the camera. A black bow adorned the little red dress she wore. When I flipped to the second picture, I bolted from the chair.

The photos fluttered to the table. I turned and hurried into the far corner of the room. "No," I said. "No, no, no." I crossed my arms and shook my head. "Nuh-uh. No fucking way."

A beam of light splashed across my arms, and I worried someone might watch me from outside. I stepped over to the window and scanned the neighboring buildings. I should have pulled the shades before looking through the wallets.

Why hadn't I done that?

Paranoia lanced through my chest. I yanked down the shades on all the windows. My eyes struggled to adjust to the reduced lighting.

A couple of years back, I lifted a wallet with some naked pictures of men. They were engaged in sexual positions, but this wasn't like that.

I flicked on the kitchen light and returned to the table. I didn't sit, however. I spread out the photographs. Each picture was more disturbing than the previous one.

Who did this type of thing to a little girl?

I scooped up the pictures and set them in the shredder. They sat on the rail, waiting for the steel teeth to tear through them. My finger hovered over the Start button.

The right decision would have been to call the police. I'm no Dudley Do Right, but the photographs were something the cops should know about. Of course, I would have to explain how I came into possession of the wallet.

"I found it," I said to myself.

I wanted to try the words on for size. Coming from my mouth, they sounded unbelievable. I cleared my throat and tried again.

"I found it." As an afterthought, I added, "In an alley."

I shook my head. The cops wouldn't believe it. Why would they? I had a history of theft, and I'd been arrested for possession of stolen property before. If I didn't believe the story, there was no way they would.

My finger rubbed the Start button. It was the right choice. Just press the damn button and send those horrible images through the shredder. Then I could get back to my life and pretend I never saw them.

"Shit."

I stood and moved to the corner of my apartment. My fingers ran through my hair.

The police had a lot of labels—arrogant, condescending, and brutal—but they weren't stupid. Any story I could concoct about that wallet would incriminate me.

Would they forgive my theft if it led to the arrest of a pedophile?

I put my head in the corner and closed my eyes. It was something I did often while in jail, and it was a practice I developed while growing up in the foster home system. It made me feel safe.

Maybe if it was just one pickpocketing incident, but I'd gotten away with many thefts recently. Calling the cops about this would alert them I was working downtown again, and they'd suspect me of any reports of stolen wallets and purses. If they showed enough of the marks my photo, one was bound to pick me out. I'd be nailed cold.

I pushed myself from the corner and eyed the shredder. I've erased other horrible images from my mind, but could I pretend I never saw those awful pictures?

Did I want to do that? Could I abandon a kid?

"You can't help," I said. "You're not Batman."

I wasn't abused like that girl, but I grew up alone in the system and made it out okay. Maybe this kid wasn't even in the system? Hell, she's probably growing up in a home everyone deems safe and loving.

My jaw tightened. That meant I had only one option.

As I crossed the room, I said, "What the hell are you doing?"

I removed the images from the shredder but didn't look at them. I put them upside down on the table. I crossed my arms and thought about the type of person who would have pictures like that. Was he the person in the photos with the kid?

A plan formed then. It came in rough starts and stops. But the idea seemed ridiculous. It wasn't what I did. I stole. What I was about to do was the opposite of that.

I grabbed a towel from the kitchen and then rubbed each picture. As I did, I tried to avoid looking at their images. I wanted to ensure none of my fingerprints were anywhere to be found. I was rubbing off someone else's, too, but that couldn't be helped. I needed to make sure it kept me out of this mess.

Using the towel to hold the photographs was awkward, but I eventually got them tucked back into the pocket they were initially in. Then I pulled out the businessman's driver's license and studied it.

Troy Pembrook smiled in the photograph. His skin was less tanned when it was taken, but his blue eyes sparkled. How could a guy who looked so successful do something so monstrous?

Weren't pedophiles creepy older men who lived in basement apartments? This guy looked like he hung out at Chamber of Commerce meetings.

I copied the information from his license and then studied his face for a few minutes. When I was sure I would never forget him, I rubbed my fingerprints off the laminated card and slipped it back into the wallet.

***

The following day, I drove through Troy Pembrook's South Hill neighborhood. It was in an older development along the city limits but still very exclusive. The newer planned communities would have gates and codes to keep out people like me.

My dented, out-of-date Chevy Malibu clashed with the large homes and manicured lawns. Most cars in the neighborhood were safely tucked in three-car garages, but the vehicles parked in the driveways shined and likely carried price tags beyond the region's median household.

When I found Pembrook's McMansion, I cruised by without stopping. I looped twice more through the neighborhood until I finally found the courage to stop. I parked a few houses away and walked back.

I softly knocked on the front door. This neighborhood seemed built to intimidate interlopers like me.

Embarrassed by my timidity, I knocked louder a second time. I pulled my shoulders back and thrust out my chin.

A woman in her late thirties opened the door. A gray sweatshirt hung low over spandex pants and sweat glistened on her smooth forehead. "Yes?"

"Is Mr. Pembrook home?"

She considered my dark suit and shined black shoes. "He's at the office."

"The office." I snapped my fingers. Nothing in Pembrook's wallet had revealed where he worked. "Of course."

Her eyes narrowed. "What do you want with Troy?"

"We have some business."

"So you came to our home?" She shook her head. "Why are you really here?"

A tiny voice behind her asked, "Mommy?"

The woman turned and revealed the girl from the photographs. She looked warily at me.

"Gabby, go back inside. I'll be there in a minute."

The child hesitated. Her eyes remained locked on me. "*Now*, Gabby."

When the girl left, the woman faced me. "What's this about?"

"I'm here to see your husband."

"That didn't answer my question. What's your name?"

I motioned into the house. "Was that your daughter?"

"You don't get to know that." She stepped back and started to close the door.

"Wait," I said.

She paused and stared through a small opening in the doorway. "What?"

"Are you aware of what your husband is doing with your daughter?"

Anger flashed in her eyes before she slammed the door

shut.

***

Spokane is not a small city; it's over a quarter million people. You can bump into the same person twice if you try, but it's not a guarantee. You've got to concentrate on the area of town where you first saw them, but it still doesn't make it a certainty. All that effort could result in a monumental waste of time.

I did not know if Pembrook was on his way to his office when I stole his wallet. He might not even work downtown for all I knew. Perhaps he was in the mall to buy a gift for his wife. Although, he wasn't carrying a shopping bag that day. Maybe he had lunch there. The mall had plenty of dining options. Or it could have been a business meeting of some kind.

If Pembrook was on his way back to the office from lunch, there were plenty of buildings for him to choose from. I'd be hard-pressed to find him on that sidewalk again.

Was the mall close to his destination or far? If it was close, the likelihood of contact increased significantly. The more I thought about the latter option, the less I felt it was likely. Spokanites didn't walk far like those in other cities. It seemed a habit born of yesteryear when parking was plentiful. Now that it was tighter, the residents complained more, but wouldn't walk any further. They would drive ten blocks and fight for a parking spot instead of just walking.

Humans are creatures of habit, but Troy Pembrook wasn't guaranteed to follow the same route to and from his office building daily. Perhaps he was of the mindset to take a new way each day to keep his mind and attitude fresh. It was something I tried to do whenever I returned home. Maybe he did the same. Which meant I could squat for days at that corner where I picked his pocket and not know Pembrook was happily using alternate routes to get to his destination.

Perhaps he was sick. Maybe he changed his habits after his wallet was stolen—that was a possibility. Perhaps his wife told him about my visit, and he realized the thief was coming for him about the pictures. There was no telling what Troy Pembrook might do.

Of course, society made searching for people easier with the invention of the internet. I didn't own a computer, but the library had a host of them for the public's use. I stopped at the downtown branch and waited for one to open up. When it did, I entered Troy Pembrook's name and waited for the search results.

There were several Troy Pembrook's nationwide, so I narrowed the search by including Spokane in the search bar. Almost nothing came back—just some city records pertaining to permits pulled on his South Hill home. I pulled the assessor's record on his home and found only Troy Pembrook's name. Married couples usually showed up on the official record. Perhaps it was nothing and Pembrook purchased the house before he was married. Yet maybe there was something nefarious underneath it all and he was a controlling jerk and listed only himself. I wanted to think the latter.

I continued my search and found nothing relating to his job. No news reports. Not even a Facebook account. That surprised me. I leaned back and crossed my arms. Most folks have something on the internet unless they tried hard to stay off. It required significant effort. I knew because I tried to remain a digital shadow. My arrest records were public, and those showed up whenever I searched my name. I did that occasionally. Other than those unfortunate moments, I was an internet ghost.

Maybe Pembrook didn't want his name spread around the World Wide Web. Perhaps guys that abused their daughters preferred to keep a low profile. Had I gotten his wife's name, I could have searched for her, but she had kept that information to herself.

I stared at the computer monitor for a moment. I wasn't a detective, so guessing the next move felt foreign. I was a thief. This clearly wasn't my strong suit. I deleted my search request and closed the internet browser. I wouldn't find Pembrook clacking away on a keyboard. I had to go with what I knew.

***

I returned to Troy Pembrook's neighborhood later that night.

Several couples were out for evening walks. I smiled benignly and waved, but that didn't satisfy their curiosity. One gentleman stopped and turned around to watch my car cruise through his neighborhood.

At Pembrook's house, a black BMW sat in the driveway. A car hadn't been there earlier. Did Mrs. Pembrook park hers inside the attached two-car garage? Did her husband also park inside, meaning this sedan belonged to a guest? I continued past the house and out of the neighborhood.

I found a nearby McDonald's and stopped for dinner. I wasn't a budget victim, but I didn't feel like dropping three bills on a meal tonight. My attitude was sour and spending money on a fancy dish seemed wasteful. I hung out there so long my French fries grew cold, and my milk shake became runny. When darkness fell, it was about nine.

Back at Pembrook's house, the same BMW was in the
driveway. It likely did not belong to a guest, I decided.
There was no need to hang around any further. I'd come
back early in the morning.

I wended my way out of the development. Blue and
red lights lit up the night as I pulled onto the arterial.
There was no hesitation in deciding on a course of action.
My car would never outrun a patrol car. Even if I had the
fastest car in Spokane, it would never outdistance a police
radio. I pulled to the side of the road, turned off the
engine, and put my hands on the steering wheel.

A spotlight from the patrol car highlighted my car and
rendered the rearview mirror useless.

"And here they come," I muttered.

Two figures approached, one on each side of my car.
Their shadows moved in the side mirrors.

There are two ways to handle cops. Fight every time
you encounter them or stand still until they've sniffed
you and get bored. Some of my friends learned the hard
way.

The officer on the driver's side leaned down near my
window. "Good evening. I'm Officer Ervin with the
Spokane Police Department. Do you know why we
stopped you?"

While the officer spoke, his gaze swept over my car's
interior. Even though I couldn't see the other cop, I'm
sure he was doing the same thing.

"No, sir," I said. "I signaled."

"Suspicious circumstances." Ervin continued to
inspect my car visually.

"Excuse me?"

His gaze settled on me. "You're suspicious."

I gripped the steering wheel tighter. "Why is that?"

"You're not from the neighborhood."

"How do you know?"

Officer Ervin snapped his fingers. "License, registration, and proof of insurance."

I furrowed my brow but kept my hands on the wheel. "You profiled my car."

The cop waggled his fingers. "Your documents."

"I have every right to be in that neighborhood."

Ervin's lip curled and his eyes darkened. "The fuck you do."

His sudden change in demeanor made me hesitant to argue further. "My paperwork is in the glove box."

"Nice and easy."

I reached over, and the other officer pointed his flashlight at the glove compartment. He was speaking into his shoulder microphone as he did so.

After rummaging through the glove box, I located my registration and insurance. I straightened and pulled my driver's license from my pocket. I handed the documents to Officer Ervin.

"Yo," the cop from the passenger side called. "Dispatch advises the registered owner is Scott McGrath. Clear DOL. Two felony theft convictions, though."

Ervin rested an elbow on my car door. "A thief?"

I looked away from his accusatory glance. "Reformed."

"What are you doing in this neighborhood?"

"House shopping."

"Not in here. We don't allow felons."

Shit, I thought. This was *his* neighborhood. "Yes, sir. I understand."

"If you come back, we won't have a pleasant conversation like we're having now. Understand?"

"Yes, sir."

Ervin tossed my driver's license, registration, and insurance card into my lap. "Get the fuck out of here and don't come back."

***

The next morning, I returned to Pembrook's neighborhood—sort of. Even staying outside of the development was a risk. I assumed Officer Ervin's shift was over, and he was safely tucked into his bed.

If he wasn't, he'd soon return home in his civilian car. He couldn't legally contact me. If I saw him approaching, I'd drive away. If he wanted to make a stink about it later while in uniform, I'd let him. I hadn't stayed at the address listed on my driver's license in two years. The system did not know where I currently lived.

I parked forty yards outside the development's entrance and watched the exiting traffic. My eyes hurt as if sandpaper were on the inside of my lids. I sipped some lukewarm coffee I purchased earlier to keep my edge. I hadn't slept much since seeing the photographs of the girl.

Eventually, a black BMW stopped at the edge of the development. When traffic cleared, the car turned in my direction. Troy Pembrook was behind the wheel, and he seemed to sing along with the radio. I couldn't sleep, and that bastard didn't have a care in the world. Why wasn't he upset he lost his wallet? He had to know someone out there had his pictures. Was he assuming the thief would simply take the money and burn the incriminating evidence? Maybe that's what others would have done. Perhaps that's what I should have done.

I flipped a U-turn and was rewarded with a horn blast and tires screeching.

Pembrook drove down Regal Street. His head bobbed, and his hands tapped the steering wheel. At a stoplight, it appeared as if he were playing a set of air drums. I wanted to get out of my car, walk up to his window, and yell at him for being a monster.

That wouldn't bring the type of satisfaction I truly wanted.

He turned on Twenty-ninth Avenue and sped around a couple of cars. For a moment, I thought he might have seen me trailing behind him. My heart skipped a beat, and I panicked. I raced to catch up to him. Once I got closer, he was again playing the air drums. He wasn't trying to evade me; he was just a shitty driver.

When we made it downtown, he pulled into the parking garage for the Western Bank Building. I couldn't find a spot, so I abandoned my car in a commercial loading zone and ran back to the garage.

Pembrook's car wasn't on the first floor. I ran up the stairwell to the second and watched him yank open the glass door to enter the building. A moment later, he turned the corner and disappeared inside.

I raced to the door and jerked it open. Even though I wore a suit, my frantic behavior called too much attention to me. I needed to get control of myself, but I couldn't risk losing sight of Pembrook.

He stood at the bank of elevators with his shoulders pulled back and head held high. As I neared, I could hear him singing to himself. "It doesn't make a difference if we're naked or not."

I hated Bon Jovi, but even I knew that wasn't the correct lyric.

Pembrook tapped his toe and nodded his head. He mumbled the rest of the words after that.

When the elevator doors opened, he stepped in and

pressed the button for his floor. I expected him to hold the door or ask if I was getting in. Instead, he averted his eyes until the doors began closing. Then he glanced at me and smiled—the bastard.

Perhaps I should have jumped into the elevator and rode up with him. Then there would be no question where he worked. But I didn't want to be that close to him. As much as I dreamed about physically hurting him, that wasn't me.

The floor counter ticked upward. The numbers climbed to seventeen before stopping. I pressed the Up arrow, and the doors to another elevator opened. I stepped in, pressed a button, and tried to get that damn Bon Jovi song out of my head.

Naked or not. The fucking moron.

Less than a minute later, I stepped into the lobby of Kent and Wallace Financial Investments. Soft music drifted in the background of a professionally decorated office.

A young woman sat behind an enormous mahogany counter. A brass nameplate announced her as *Rene*. She smiled politely. "Sir?"

I frowned as I held Troy Pembrook's wallet up. "A guy dropped this a couple of blocks back. He was already on the elevator by the time I caught up to him."

Rene reached for the wallet, but I curled it into my hand. Her brow furrowed with confusion.

"There are some disturbing pictures in here."

The receptionist set her hand on the desk, and concern registered on her face. "You looked inside?"

"Had to. In case I didn't find the guy who lost it."

Her eyes locked onto the wallet. I pulled it back slightly, and she stood, a fish on the line.

"I wouldn't have opened it otherwise," I said. "You

understand."

"Of course." She sounded almost breathless in anticipation of knowing what was inside. "Who's it belong to?"

"Some guy named Pembrook." I handed her the billfold. "You won't like what you see."

Rene opened the wallet. She flicked through the bills that added up to one hundred eighty-six dollars. Her thumb dragged over the credit cards.

"It's all there," I said.

"I'm not accusing you of anything, sir."

I tapped the pocket holding the pictures. "You might want to look inside."

She cocked her head.

"Or maybe not," I said.

Rene slid the photographs out. She flipped through the first couple, then clutched the rest to her chest. Her face grew white, and she swallowed with difficulty.

I leaned on the counter and lowered my voice. "What do you think we should do about this?"

She blinked several times before hurriedly tucking the pictures back into the wallet. "I should call someone."

"Pembrook?"

"Oh, no." Rene emphatically shook her head. "Not now."

"Misters Kent and Wallace then? What do you think they would do about it?"

The receptionist glanced about. "They'll fire him, I guess," she whispered. "What else could they do?"

"Do you think that's enough?" I touched the edge of the wallet. "She's a little girl."

Rene's face hardened. "We should call the police."

I nodded. "That's probably for the best."

She grabbed the phone and stabbed three buttons.

When someone answered, Rene said, "Ah, yes. I'd like to report—" Her eyes clouded as she searched for the words.

"Child pornography," I suggested.

"Child pornography," Rene said into the phone. "Uh-huh. Yes, ma'am. One of our employees has it in his wallet." She looked at me and nodded. "We have it now." She lowered her head. "A citizen found the wallet outside and returned it to our office. He followed the owner. Yes. He's here now. The employee, too. Yes."

I thumbed toward the restroom. "I'm going to step around the corner."

Rene nodded, then lowered her head to concentrate on the dispatcher. "Yes, ma'am, I'm still here. We understand. We won't alert him. No, we understand. We'll wait here. Yes. Okay."

I headed down the hallway. Before I got to the restroom, I looked back at the receptionist's desk. Rene wasn't looking in my direction. I entered the stairwell and quietly shut the door.

***

The cafe in the Western Bank Building's lobby serves a wonderful Ethiopian blend. I sipped my coffee and read a left-behind copy of *The Wall Street Journal*—the perfect accessory for someone in my profession. Overhead, some bland jazz music played.

I wasn't through the national news section when two uniformed officers entered the lobby. They didn't bother approaching the elevators. Instead, they chatted and cast intimidating glances at those of us trying to spend a few quiet moments enjoying our coffee.

A man in a sport coat and jeans entered the building

and walked up to the uniforms. He whispered to the officers then the three of them headed toward the elevators. It wasn't hard to make the latecomer as a detective.

Once the three men vanished from sight, I could have taken off. I probably should have left the Western Bank Building after dropping off the wallet. Part of me wanted to see this through. I've never given too much belief in karma, but if there was ever a time to hope the scales would balance out, this was one.

I looked up expectedly every time the elevator doors opened. After a while, I stopped getting my hopes up. I finished my coffee and ordered a chai tea as a replacement. I folded *The Wall Street Journal* and moved it to the side. I opened a copy of *The Inlander*, Spokane's independent newspaper. I read a sordid article about a war of words between the mayor and sheriff about a homeless camp growing east of town.

An elevator opened, and Troy Pembrook stepped out with his head bowed. His hands were cuffed behind his back. The two uniformed officers flanked both sides of him. Pembrook's air of confidence was gone.

The detective brought up the rear. He carried a clear Ziploc bag in his left hand. Inside was Pembrook's wallet.

The lobby quieted. It seemed as if even the jazz musicians coming through the lobby speakers paused the song they were playing. Everyone stopped what they were doing to watch the procession.

I abandoned my newspaper and chai tea to follow the men outside.

The detective said something to the officers before heading toward his car. The two uniforms put Pembrook into the back of their car. One of them even put a guiding hand on his head so he wouldn't accidentally conk it. What a lovely gesture from our law enforcement community.

A crowd of us gathered on the sidewalk to watch the whole arrest play out. When Pembrook looked our way from the backseat, none of us bothered to pretend to have somewhere else to be. His eyes met mine, yet there was no recognition.

If I had hoped for a moment of vindication, none was coming.

The patrol car pulled from the curb.

I turned and bumped into a well-dressed man whose gaze was still on the patrol car. He smiled and apologized. "My bad." He lifted his hands in concession.

"Happens all the time," I said.

The man nodded once, then went toward Riverfront Park. I went the opposite direction.

When I was alone later that night, I learned the well-dressed man was named Ethan Criddle and, according to his driver's license, he lived on the north side. Criddle also had several credit cards, sixty-three dollars in cash, and four bright-white business cards that identified him as a U.S. Marshal.

Prologue to Mayhem

Detective James Morgan squatted next to Roy Utt. "Now, what's this about?"

Roy slumped with his back against The Well, a dumpy bar decaying on the corner of Washington Street and Second Avenue. He wore a Chicago Bulls jersey over a dingy white T-shirt, greasy blue jeans, and one black Converse high top. On his other foot was a dirty, pink sock. The second shoe was nowhere to be found.

Everything seemed to sag on Roy—his eyelids, cheeks, shoulders, and even his fingers. The pale man had spent the last six months in the Airway Heights Corrections Center. Based on Roy's history, immediately upon release, he likely got high. Roy wasn't the type to use a period of incarceration to turn his life around.

The junkie mumbled something and lazily waved a limp hand about.

Morgan looked up to Detective Nayla Senai. "Hey."

The tall black woman turned his way. She'd been concentrating on something across the street.

Morgan motioned to the still babbling Roy. "You getting any of this?"

"Wasn't paying attention."

"What're you looking at?"

Senai jerked her head toward two shabbily dressed white men huddled together on the opposite sidewalk. One of them held a cell phone as if filming the detectives' interaction with Roy. "Ever seen them before?"

"A couple of dead beats. Friends of this guy." The

detective leaned in to hear Roy better and caught a whiff of the man. "Christ," he muttered and stepped back. Roy smelled of feces and urine. His face was dirty, and his hair appeared to have been unwashed for several days.

Morgan kicked the junkie's single Converse shoe. "Speak up, Roy."

"The camera," Senai reminded.

Morgan kicked Roy's shoe a second time. "And make sure they can hear it across the street."

Roy widened his eyes. It seemed the man did so with great willpower. His gaze swept from Morgan to Senai, then it took a skyward arc before returning to Morgan. The junkie licked his lips and, with substantial effort, clearly and deliberately said, "Handbrake."

Senai cocked her head. "Like for a car?"

Morgan straightened. That was a name he hadn't heard in years.

The bar's back door thunked open, and a woman in her sixties popped her head out. Her wrinkled face pinched with apparent displeasure. "How long before you wrap this up?"

Morgan lifted his chin in the direction from which she came. "Go back inside, Elva."

"Please," Senai added. "We'll only be a few minutes more."

Elva Lightly stepped outside to eye Roy. "You all are affecting my business."

"Nobody can see back here," Morgan said. "There aren't any windows."

"Handbrake," Roy repeated and threw his hand as if making some unknown point.

Elva pursed her wrinkled lips. "Hell, not him, too."

"What do you mean?" Senai asked.

"It's the topic of the day." Elva thumbed toward the

building. "The idiots in there are raising their beers to Hardy Fry. It's not like they even knew the bastard. Not that I'm complaining."

"Sounds like you are," Morgan said.

Elva's eyes narrowed. "No need to be smart about it, Morgan."

"What's going on with Hardy?" he asked.

"He's dying. The man ain't supposed to make it through the weekend."

Morgan glanced at Senai, then down to the junkie.

"How'd you hear about this, Roy?"

He muttered something incomprehensible.

"Everybody's talking about it," Elva said. "They're treating it like it's a presidential calamity."

Senai glanced at Morgan. "Who's Hardy Fry?"

Elva interrupted. "How long's this gonna take, Morgan? I got customers who get jittery knowing the cops are around."

"It takes as long as it takes," Morgan said absently. His attention remained on Roy.

The older woman huffed once then reentered the bar. The door slammed behind her.

Senai looked questioningly at her partner. "You going to tell me about Hardy Fry?"

Morgan pulled out his cell phone. "The guy's a piece of shit. What more do you need to know?"

***

The Dodge Charger sped along Sprague Avenue. Morgan rested his wrist over the top of the steering wheel. "Hardy Fry was a wheelman."

Senai cocked her head.

"He drove getaway."

"Ah." She glanced out the passenger window. "A wheelman. So, he's a criminal."

"Well, yeah. You think I'd call a citizen a piece of shit?"

Senai cast a disbelieving sideways glance.

Morgan waved her off. "Whatever. The point is Hardy started driving getaway cars before you or I were ever born."

"Hard to believe."

"Why's that?"

Senai eyed him. "You're old."

Morgan frowned.

He changed lanes without signaling and zoomed around a slow-moving minivan. They passed through the intersection of Havana Road, the edge of Spokane proper, and passed into the city of Spokane Valley.

"Where are we going?" Senai asked. "Not that I mind a road trip on a Friday afternoon."

"We're going to see Hardy Fry."

Senai's eyebrows rose with curiosity. "You know this man?"

"I know of him. Some of the old guys in the department talked about him like he was a legend. I haven't heard his name in years. Maybe even a decade."

Morgan sped through a yellow light.

"What are we going to do?"

"What do you think? We're going to see who's paying their respects."

"And you know where he's staying?"

"That was the call I made."

***

"What's this happy horseshit?" Morgan asked.

Senai leaned forward in the passenger seat. "Looks like a celebration."

A large crowd of about a hundred people gathered in the parking lot of The Red Apple Nursing Home. All ages and ethnicities were represented. Many held handmade signs. One proclaimed *We Love U, Hardy!* Another advised *Outrun the Devil, Handbrake!* Morgan had no idea behind the meaning of *Fry Me to the Moon!*

Morgan parked in the fire lane and climbed out. A moment later, Senai was by his side.

"The news is here." She discreetly motioned toward a white news van on the opposite side of the parking lot.

"Jackals," Morgan said. "How's this newsworthy?"

He scanned the crowd looking for faces of anyone he might have contacted over the years. He finally found a familiar face. "You gotta be kidding me."

"What?" Senai searched for whomever Morgan identified. "Who?"

"Follow me."

Leaning against the back of a late-model Oldsmobile was a heavy-set white man. His hands rested on the wooden cane in front of him. The man appeared to be in his early eighties. He wore faded blue jeans, a gray WSU sweatshirt, and brown loafers. In a leather paddle holster on his right hip was a revolver.

Standing next to the man was a woman about a decade younger. She was dressed stylishly in dark slacks and a white sweater. Her silver hair was short and recently cut.

The couple watched the cheering crowd with open disgust.

As Morgan and Senai approached, the older man turned slightly to eye him. His revolt faded and was replaced by a genial smile. "Well, I'll be."

Morgan extended his hand. "Alan Tannenhill, you old

dog, how the hell are you?"

"I'm fine. Just fine." The older man slipped his hand into Morgan's. "You met my wife, Helen?"

"I haven't."

"Helen," the older man said, "this spry, young fella is Jimmy Morgan. He was a patrolman for a time. We met on a couple of scenes."

Morgan didn't bother to correct Alan about the familiar use of his first name. He introduced Senai, and everyone exchanged their initial pleasantries. "Alan was in Major Crimes," Morgan told Senai. "He retired a couple years after I came on."

"Is that so?" Senai asked.

Alan eyed Morgan. "I see your name in the paper, kid. Yours, too, Nayla." He turned his attention to the crowd in the parking lot. "Can you believe this nonsense?"

"It's disrespectful," Helen said, "celebrating a criminal in this manner."

Alan tapped his cane on the asphalt. "People have been doing it for years. Don't forget they celebrated Bonnie and Clyde."

Helen shook her head. "Billy the Kid and Jesse James, too."

"And they were all killers." Alan pursed his lips.

"Far as I heard," Morgan said, "Hardy Fry never killed anybody."

"I wouldn't bet on that."

Helen hooked her arm into her husband's. "What's this world coming to when we honor this type of behavior?"

Morgan asked, "What brought you down?"

Alan's lip curled. "I got a call Hardy was on the way out. I wanted to be here when he met his maker. What about you?"

"Word is on the street." Morgan motioned toward a cameraman filming the crowd. "Looks like it's further than that now. Anyway, I figured there would be a few who might want to pay some respects. Thought it would be worth seeing if any came. Maybe we could snag a couple and get some easy arrests."

Alan clucked his tongue. "Padding the stats. Same old game."

"Same old department," Morgan said.

"Well, there's a few mopes already here."

"Yeah?"

The older man motioned toward two gray-haired men standing together. They were hunched with age and seemed slightly bewildered by the size of the crowd. "Hammerhead Hendrick and Two-Pistols Pauly. They were a couple of losers from back in the day."

Senai said, "Morgan said this Hardy character was never arrested."

"Don't get him started," Helen said.

Alan tapped his cane. "We had him plenty. Sometimes we should have had him dead to rights."

Morgan lifted an eyebrow. "What happened?"

"It's going to sound stupid." Alan rubbed his chin before continuing. "I think it was luck."

Morgan and Senai glanced at each other.

"See? I told you." Alan jammed his cane once more into the asphalt. "The feeble musings of an old man, I know what you're thinking, but Hardy was involved in a lot of crimes. We knew about some of them. There had to be more we didn't. A guy can't do that much without something in his corner."

"Luck," Morgan said.

"You think it was supernatural?" Senai asked.

The retired detective sighed. It sounded raspy, like his

own health might be failing. "Not luck as if the gods were looking out for him. Think of it as probability. Statistics, you know?" Alan looked to his wife, then the detectives. "Look at it this way. Flipping a coin is a fifty-fifty proposition. Heads or tails. You flip it once, and it comes up heads. What're the chances it comes up heads the next time?"

"Fifty percent," Senai said.

Alan smiled. "That's right. Now, let's say you flip it five times in a row, and it comes up heads each time. What's the probability that it comes up heads the sixth time?"

"Still fifty percent," Senai said.

Alan eyed Morgan. "She's a smart cookie."

"Tell me about it." Morgan's eyes narrowed. "But the probability of all those flips coming up heads has to be minuscule, right."

"Sure it is," Alan said, "but it still doesn't affect what happens next. The probability of each flip is independent of the previous flip. Understand?"

"So you're saying," Senai said, "Hardy Fry's legendary career is built upon a long string of good luck?"

"Why not? There are plenty of dirtballs who couldn't catch a break." Alan pointed to the two gray-haired men. "Hammerhead and Two-Pistols got arrested plenty of times for rips that should have gone smoothly. If you ask them why, they'd chalk it up to bad luck. Hell, I always thought so."

Morgan tried to hide his skepticism, but Alan saw it.

"Don't believe me, kid? It's yin and yang. It's karma. The universe is all about balance." Alan waved a hand about. "It has to put all that good luck somewhere, and I think it dropped it on Hardy Fry."

Helen leaned toward Senai. "I told you not to get him started."

The four of them turned to watch the crowd as it tried to break into a choppy rendition of "American Pie." The group seemed intent on mangling the words about driving a Chevy to a levy.

"How long are you going to stay here?" Morgan asked.

"We've got nothing but time," Alan said. "I'd like nothing better than to be in the vicinity when Hardy Fry's luck finally runs out. How about you?"

Morgan considered the crowd. Those cheering for the infamous Handbrake Hardy Fry weren't hardened criminals. They seemed to be those peripheral types who show up to events because they don't have much else going on in their lives. Besides the two crooked geezers Alan mentioned, it didn't seem like there were many criminals in the crowd.

"I think I had it wrong," Morgan said. "It looks like we made a trip for nothing."

Alan eyed him. "You might leave too soon, kid. Hardy Fry had a strange pull to some. Why don't you stick around and see who shows up?"

Morgan turned to Senai. "What do you think?"

She smiled. "It's a sunny day. There are worse ways to spend it."

The crowd continued to sing out of tune about some good old boys drinking their whiskey and rye.

Morgan crossed his arms. "All right, then. We'll stay. Let's see if anyone we know is stupid enough to show up."

The Reunion of Back Road Bobby and Transmission Jack

Bobby Tobeck pushed his baseball hat back on his head and eyed the man sitting across from him. "Aren't you gonna eat?"

"Ain't hungry." Jack Tobeck angrily shoved away the oval plate containing country-fried steak, mashed potatoes, and green beans. It clanked against his ceramic coffee cup.

The two men sat in a booth at the Shari's on Sullivan Road. Nearby customers noisily scraped their plates with metal utensils as they carried on louder than necessary conversations. Overhead, some sappy love song played. Bobby didn't know what it was, nor did he care. He didn't care for music and tended to ignore it.

"You seemed hungry a few minutes ago," Bobby said. He sawed through his own country-fried steak. "I thought this was your favorite when Mom used to make it."

"You don't know nothing about me."

That was a true statement; he barely knew the man. Jack had gone away when Bobby was seventeen. Bobby stopped his train of thought. That last statement wasn't accurate, however.

Transmission Jack Tobeck had gone to prison when Bobby was a junior in high school. "Going away" was the euphemism he used when talking with citizens or respectable women he hoped to bed. The runaround girls knew about his dad. Most of their fathers had done time, too.

Jack was recently released from Walla Walla State Penitentiary after serving twenty-two years. He was sentenced to forty, but good behavior and a recent stroke earned him early parole.

Unfortunately, the brain attack limited the use of his left arm and smeared that side of his face. Not that anyone was going to be concerned with Transmission Jack now. He was seventy-two years old, gray, and unstable. The metal walker positioned next to the booth was a constant reminder of his frailty.

"Want me to cut it for you?" Bobby asked.

"Want me to punch your teeth in?" Jack's words weren't crisp with anger like they were when he was younger. Instead, his father sounded mushy like an overripe apple, if such a thing could talk.

"Okay, Jack. Take it easy."

"I don't like that."

"What don't you like?"

"You calling me that."

Bobby chuckled. "Well, I ain't calling you Pops, and I sure as hell won't call you Dad. That ship has sailed."

"I'm still your father." It wasn't said with love or respect, but rather ownership.

The man had grown smaller while in prison. Bobby corrected himself; shrunk was probably a better word. Jack had *shrunk* over the years.

Jack Tobeck once stood a couple of inches shy of six feet. Now, he'd lost a couple more due to time and curvature of the spine. Jack could no longer look down on his son and instead had to look him directly in the eye with that sloppy left side of his face.

When Bobby was a boy, Jack was exceptionally irate, which was probably why his young mother had fled one evening and left her son to the care of her older and heavy-handed husband. Jack was feared among those who lived their lives outside of polite society. Drivers were usually seen as amiable types, but Transmission Jack Tobeck wasn't one of them.

Prison and old age seemed to have tamed the man. Maybe his bark was always worse than his bite, but Bobby was just too young to know the difference back then.

Bobby scooped some mashed potatoes from his plate. "This have something to do with that call?"

"What if it does?" His father turned away from the table to stare out the window. "Like you'd give two shits."

After they'd ordered, Jack received a call on his cell phone. He got up without a word and clanged away with the walker. His left leg moved awkwardly like a lame horse, although Bobby never remembered his father being a graceful sort. He stifled a laugh as Jack left. The old man looked hapless now with his black wool sweater, gray polyester slacks, and brown loafers. Jack was about as threatening as a toothless Chihuahua.

The old man returned shortly after the server delivered their plates. He dropped into the booth and moped.

"You're right," Bobby said. "About me not caring, I mean. Maybe you should tell your therapist, though. See what she thinks of your crappy attitude."

His father scoffed but didn't look away from the window. "Like I'm telling that bitch anything. She'll tattle to the court."

"Maybe it'll help to talk." Bobby snickered. "Doesn't your testosterone go all to hell at your age? Make you all weepy like a woman? I've seen the commercials."

Jack sneered, but it quickly faded. His gaze grew distant, and tears welled in his eyes. He swallowed with some difficulty and turned further away from his son.

Bobby considered making another crack about low testosterone, but that felt like kicking a man when he was down. He shoveled some creamy potatoes into his mouth. He hadn't finished chewing them before he stabbed a few beans and shoved them in as well. Better to keep chewing than cracking wise. He studied his father as the old man watched a souped-up Honda race northbound on Sullivan.

"Goddamned rice burners," Jack muttered. The good side of his lip curled as his eyes tracked the car. "Noisy sumbitches. Good for nothings."

Bobby cut another piece of meat and slipped it into his mouth.

Jack's gaze shifted to him. "Knock that shit off."

"Mmph?" Bobby grunted.

"You and that moaning." Jack's scowl deepened. "I figured you'd have outgrown that nonsense by now."

Bobby occasionally moaned while he ate. It was an unintentional habit he had developed in childhood. He delighted in food, whether it was the greasy joy of country-fried steak or the wonderfully clean taste of nigiri sushi.

Jack continued. "It sounds like you're—" He turned toward the window and shook his head again. "Whatever. It's just gross."

Bobby sliced free another piece of meat. "You tell me what's going on—" He stuck the country-fried steak into his mouth and exaggeratedly moaned. Jack's head jerked back toward him, and his scowl deepened. Bobby smiled in the cruel way his father had taught him as a boy. "Or I'll take you home. I'm sure Shawna will be happy to have your grumpy ass back so soon."

Jack inhaled deeply and stuck his tongue underneath his upper lip to stop it from shaking. "It's Hardy Fry."

Bobby finished chewing while waiting for his father to elaborate. When Jack didn't, Bobby said, "Handbrake?"

"He's dying."

"No shit." Bobby worked on the meat. "The guy's a million years old."

"Ninety-one," Jack said with hardening eyes. "And show some goddamned respect."

Bobby slipped another bite into his mouth. This time he didn't moan.

Jack eyed him.

"Now what?" Bobby asked through a mouthful.

"How can you eat at a time like this?"

"I'm hungry."

"I just told you Hardy is dying."

Bobby dropped his knife and fork onto his plate. "How's that affect me?"

"Are you retarded?" Even with that sloppy left side of his face, Jack's disgust was evident. "The man is a legend."

"Was, Jack, was. When's the last time Hardy Fry's done anything except live on stories of forgotten glory?"

Jack turned to face his son fully, and he thunked a gnarled finger against the table. "No one's forgotten shit. Being a legend means you did something people still talk about." He flicked his hand. "What have you ever done?"

"Besides take care of myself after you went away?"

Jack's brow furrowed, and the right side of his lips pulled back to reveal yellowed teeth. "I taught you enough."

"What'd you teach me?"

"I taught you to drive."

"Lots of parents—"

Jack smacked the table with his right hand, and the silverware clattered. He leaned forward and said through clenched teeth, "Not like I did."

Bobby grabbed his napkin and wiped his mouth. "What do you want, Jack? You wanna go see Hardy? I'll take you right now."

"What's wrong with you?"

"You said he's dying."

"We all die, moron." Jack ruefully shook his head. "Seeing the man would be disrespectful. I told you to show some respect, and then you go and say something stupid like that. No wonder you get the jobs you get."

"I do fine with my jobs."

"Fine? What's fine?"

"Fine is not serving time in the state pen."

Jack's jaw flexed several times before he spoke. "That mouth of yours."

"You're a little old to be correcting me."

"Is this how you've been all these years?"

"What's it matter to you?"

"It doesn't." Jack shook his head. "In case you haven't figured it out, a man like Hardy doesn't want people coming to see him in that godforsaken state. I should know."

"Is that right?" Bobby stared mockingly at the left side of his father's face. Jack turned and looked deeper into the restaurant, hiding the damage caused by the stroke.

"What do you think the old man would want?" Bobby asked.

"He'd want to be celebrated."

"Yeah?" Bobby chuckled. "You think you should be celebrated, too, Jack?"

His father's face reddened as he slowly turned toward him. "Fuck yourself, son."

"That's something you never see in a Hallmark card." Bobby picked up his knife and fork. "Are you suggesting we go for some beers? Maybe raise a toast to Handbrake Hardy Fry and Transmission Jack—" He said the names with dramatic flair like a club owner announcing a band taking the stage. "—so you can school me about the good, old times." Bobby pointed the fork at his father. "There weren't any good, old times for me, Jack."

"That's not what I'm saying."

"Then spit it out. What do you want?"

"I want to go with you, you stupid shit. Tomorrow morning."

Bobby shook his head. "No."

"Well, too bad because I'm riding shotgun. That's how we're celebrating Hardy's life."

"You don't get to make that decision."

"I'm your father," he said. "Hardy taught me to drive, and I taught you. I want to see how those skills earned you that stupid nickname."

"It's not stupid."

"Says you. Back Road? How'd you get that? You like it in the butt or something?"

Bobby pushed his plate away even though he was still hungry. Maybe he could get a to-go bag. "I'm gonna let Shawna deal with you. I still can't believe the state let you out and gave you a nurse—"

"You can take me home," Jack interrupted, "but I'm still going with you in the morning."

"No, you're not."

Jack smacked the table again. He pointed that damned gnarly finger at him. It had pointed at Bobby a lot when he was younger. It wasn't knobby then, and the nail hadn't yellowed, but it had much the same effect as it did now.

Bobby signaled a server. She noticed his wave and headed in their direction.

"If you don't take me," Jack said, "I'll tell everybody what my boy has been up to."

"You don't know what I've been up to."

Jack's eyes narrowed. "I know enough."

"Then you'd be a rat."

His father shrugged.

Bobby rested his arms along the edge of the table. "Like the cops would ever believe a broken-down convict like you."

"Don't forget what I went away for, moron. They'd believe me plenty if I said I was trying to make restitution." He put his good hand over his heart. "Trying to make up for their fallen brethren."

When the server neared, Bobby held up two fingers. "We need the check and a couple doggie bags."

"Not yet," Jack said. He pulled his plate toward him. "Feels like I finally got my appetite back."

***

In the morning, Bobby pulled to the curb in front of a one-story brick building in the Logan neighborhood. He drove a red and white 1984 GMC High Sierra 4X4. He dropped the truck into Park but didn't bother turning off the engine. Before he hopped out, he glanced into the rearview mirror and quickly tightened the brim curl of his baseball hat.

His father waited on the sidewalk with his nurse, Shawna Robinson. She was a petite black woman in her mid-thirties—several years younger than Bobby. She wore a pale blue nurse's uniform that looked oddly exotic—especially the comfortable white shoes with thick soles. Bobby thought so when he met her the first time a couple of days ago.

Jack Tobeck wore the same outfit he did the previous day.

Bobby hurried around the truck. "How was he this morning?"

Shawna nodded curtly. "He was fine."

"Why you asking her?" Jack asked. "It's not like I'm an imbecile."

Bobby ignored his father and kept his attention focused on Shawna. "So, no trouble?"

She pursed her lips. "Not really."

Jack grunted his displeasure before motioning toward the back of the truck. "What in the hell is that?" He shuffled over to the pickup. His left leg dragged as his walker rattled along on the concrete sidewalk.

A large wire crate sat inside the truck bed. Several straps secured it in place. Inside the crate was a large black dog that stood on a rugged plastic platform. The animal stared at the three of them.

Shawna smiled at the dog. "It's a Rottweiler."

"A big sumbitch." Jack said. He cast a sideways glance at his son. "What's it doing in there?"

Bobby leaned back against the truck but didn't take his eyes from Shawna. He smiled when he said, "That's what we're delivering."

"What's its name?" Jack asked. "Godzilla?"

"We'll be gone a few hours," Bobby said. He hoped Shawna might ask where they were going so the conversation would continue, but Jack leaned over and sniffed him.

"You smell like a French whore."

Bobby's shoulders slumped. "Christ, Jack. It's cologne."

"Who you trying to impress? The dog?"

Shawna motioned Jack toward the front of the pickup.

"Let's get you in."

The passenger door squealed when Bobby opened it. He and Shawna helped the older man into the truck. The door squealed once more when it closed. Bobby grabbed Jack's walker and tossed it unceremoniously into the truck bed.

"When will you be back?" Shawna asked.

"I'm thinking after six. Will that be a problem?"

"That'll be fine." She started toward the house.

"Hey, Shawna." Bobby extended his hand and immediately felt foolish for it. He started to pull it back. "Thank you."

She stuck her hand into his. "Of course."

Bobby felt a strange excitement touching Shawna's hand. She was small like him, and he liked that she was attractive. Maybe it was her abrupt demeanor that sent the thrill through him. It sure wasn't those damn shoes, although he did sort of like them. He watched her walk toward the house before hustling to the driver's side of the truck.

When Bobby climbed into the Chevy, Jack asked, "What's the matter with you?"

"What?"

His father thumbed toward the house. "She's black."

"Shut up."

"You think you got a shot with her? Think about some of the men she's been with."

"Leave it alone, Jack." Bobby dropped the truck into gear and pulled away from the curb.

"All I'm saying is you ain't exactly a towering oak."

"I said shut the fuck up."

Jack Tobeck was quiet for several blocks. Then he announced, "She helped me in the shower today."

"No, she didn't."

"She touched my wanger."

"Your wanger? What are you—five?"

"I didn't want to say cock, but if that's how you want to think about it, so be it."

Bobby shook his head. "Goddamn it, Jack. That's not true. She didn't touch it."

"Well, she saw it. I made sure of it, and you know that much is true."

"I don't care."

"Yeah, you do." Jack cackled. "You sure as hell do."

***

The two men rode mostly in silence until they entered downtown. They were southbound on Browne Street headed toward the freeway when they passed The House of Charity. A group of men huddled together.

"Goddamned bums," Jack said.

"They're homeless."

"Leeches on society is what they are. We should stop helping them."

"We?" Bobby asked.

That's about all the arguing he felt like doing with Jack on the subject. Pointing out his father hadn't paid taxes most of his life and had been a ward of the state's penitentiary system for more than two decades would only lead to more arguing.

Jack scowled at a man holding a *Will Work for Beer* sign. "Any man that can't help himself should be put out of society's misery. That's what I say."

"That's what you say."

"Are you mocking me?"

"Just agreeing." Bobby turned westbound onto Second Avenue.

Jack's head whipped around as he seemingly tried to understand the reason for the change in direction. "Stopping for gas?"

"No."

"Food?"

"I told you to eat before I picked you up." Bobby glanced at his father. "You ate, right?"

"I'm not a goddamned, baby. Where are we going?"

"I told you—Omak."

Jack glanced over his shoulder. "But the freeway entrance—"

"We're not taking the freeway."

"Right, the back road thing." Jack settled into his seat, then tugged on the seatbelt around his waist. "Damn, these are uncomfortable."

"Stop complaining because you're wearing it. The cops can stop me for it."

"Bullshit if they can."

"A lot's changed since you went in."

"They can't even see it."

A stoplight turned yellow up ahead, and Bobby slowed for it. When he came to a full stop, Bobby realized Jack was staring at him.

"What?"

"You could have made it."

"I know."

"Then why didn't you gun it?"

Bobby motioned over his shoulder. "I got the dog to consider."

Jack frowned. "There are two types of people in this world."

"You told me before."

"Obviously, you need to hear it again, moron."

"No, I don't, and stop calling me that."

Jack held up a finger. "There are those who think yellow means stop." He popped up a second finger. "And there are those who *know* it means to go faster."

Bobby inhaled deeply through his nose and held his breath.

Jack twisted in his seat and looked out the rear window. "What's with the dog?"

"It's what we're delivering. Now, shut up."

"You think you're the Humane Society or something?"

The light changed, and Bobby accelerated.

Jack unclicked his seatbelt. "Put on the radio."

"No."

"How come?"

"I said."

Jack pursed his lips and shook his head. "Aw, fuck this." He reached for the radio's knob.

Bobby slapped the old man's hand. "Not while I'm driving. Put on your seatbelt."

His father rubbed the back of his hand. "When'd you become such a nancy?"

"This isn't going to work. I'm taking you back."

Jack glared at him. "You'd like that, wouldn't you? Give you another opportunity to run your gums with her."

"Stop talking."

"Hell, we ain't said nothing to each other for twenty-two years. Why should we start now?" Jack crossed his arms and seethed in his seat.

Bobby didn't turn the truck around. There were only four more hours to go.

He could stand his father for one day.

***

Twenty minutes later, they entered the town of Airway Heights. It sat just west of Spokane and was the home of Fairchild Air Force Base. New retail developments lined Highway 2.

Jack's mouth hung open as he gawked about. "What the hell happened out here?"

"Prosperity." When his father didn't respond, Bobby said, "It means—"

"I know what it means, smartass. I read books." As they passed Hayford Road, Jack leaned into his window. "What's that over there? That big building?"

"The casino."

Jack glanced at Bobby. "No shit? They were just starting it when I went in." He looked back at the massive building and whistled. "Look at that bastard."

"There's two out here now."

"Two?" Jack sat up straighter and searched for the second casino. "But they're not legit, right?"

"What do you mean? Of course, they're legit."

"I mean, they're Indian casinos."

"Jesus, Jack." Bobby shook his head. "Stop talking."

His father slumped in his seat. "Probably can't get a decent broad in either one."

"Broad? Who says that?"

Jack ignored Bobby's question and watched a Volvo station wagon speed by. "It's forty-five along here, and you're doing what—" He leaned over to look at the dashboard. "Forty-three?"

"The speedometer is off a couple miles. Trust me— I'm doing forty-five."

"On the dot. The cops let you push it four miles over. They teach them that in the academy."

"No, they don't."

"Well, ain't nobody gonna say nothing. Give it some

gas."

"It's not how I drive."

Jack glanced over his shoulder. "Because of the dog?"

"Because of the law."

"Goddamned nancy." Jack crossed his arms. "I taught you better than that."

When they neared Fairchild Air Force Base, Jack said, "Did you know they used to have nukes out here?"

Bobby sniffed dismissively. "Nukes."

"Bombs, dumb ass. This place was like target numero uno for the commies."

"Not anymore."

Jack watched the guard shack pass by. "Yeah, not anymore. Life was simpler during the Cold War."

***

By the time they made the small town of Reardon, Jack's head lulled. Soon, his chin bounced against his chest, and soft snoring started.

Bobby enjoyed the quiet of Highway 2. The stretch of road beyond Airway Heights was mostly rolling farmland. There was a fair amount of eastbound traffic, though. Bobby could never be certain, but he imagined the residents of the modest communities headed to Spokane to shop. He wondered if many drove beyond Airway Heights now that it had almost everything a person might need.

He gently slowed the truck as he entered the town of Davenport so as not to awaken Jack. Unfortunately, when Bobby turned north onto Highway 25, his father snorted awake. He rubbed a finger under his nose and looked sleepily around.

"Where are we?"

"Davenport."

"Why'd you turn? This isn't the fastest way."

"Let me do the driving."

Jack leaned his head back. "Unless you're going to go up through Republic to come down on top of Omak, which don't make any sense. It'll add an hour to our trip."

Bobby didn't answer.

"This isn't how I taught you to drive. Path of least resistance. Remember?" Jack wiggled his hand back and forth before motioning toward the speedometer. "You drive like an old woman."

"Said the old man."

Jack snapped his fingers. "Listen here."

"Keep talking." Bobby rolled down his window, and the wind loudly whistled into the cab of the truck.

"You afraid of this machine?" Jack smacked the dashboard. "Goose it some."

Bobby pointed out the front window. "Look."

"What?"

"What do you see?" Bobby asked.

Jack leaned forward, and his eyes narrowed.

Half a mile ahead, a patrol car sat roadside. A deputy stood nearby with a radar gun pointed in their direction.

It took a few more seconds before Jack's eyes widened. He settled back into his seat and crossed his arms. "You got lucky."

"Uh-huh."

As they passed the Lincoln County deputy, Bobby waved and smiled.

The lawman returned the pleasantry.

"You think he'd still wave," Jack asked, "if he knew I was in here?"

Fifteen minutes later, Jack faced him. "Why didn't you come and see me?"

"You know why."

"Twenty-two years is a long time."

"Should have been forty."

"It's not like I did it on purpose."

"The court thinks you did."

Jack waved away Bobby's comment. "I meant prison. It's not like I wanted to leave you alone."

"But you did."

"You're never gonna forgive me, are you?"

Bobby rolled his lower lip down as he thought. He didn't know why he did it—pretending to think. He already knew the answer to Jack's question.

"Aw, fuck it," Jack said. "I shoulda never come along."

"Too late now."

***

They crossed the Columbia River at the Fort Spokane Campgrounds.

Jack twisted in his seat. Even from the corner of his eye, Bobby could see that mushy grin.

"Hey," Jack said, "did I ever tell you about the time Hardy took me up here? I had to have been maybe twenty-three and—"

"You told me when I was a kid."

Jack's smile melted. "Let me tell it again."

"No."

"But we're celebrating Hardy's life—you and me."

"I'm not celebrating shit. I'm working."

Jack repositioned himself and watched Fort Spokane fade away in the side mirror. "It was a nice memory, is all."

***

Bobby pulled into a gas station at Fruitland.

"I'm gonna hit the head," Bobby said, "then top off the tank."

"Good idea." Jack's door popped open with a squeal. "Grab my walker, will ya?"

Bobby slid from the cab. "Grab it yourself."

He walked casually into the store and waved at the woman behind the cash register. Phyllis was in her late sixties with tousled white hair and genial blue eyes.

"Look who's back," she said. "Where've you been?"

"On the road." Bobby motioned toward the restroom. "Is it open?"

She looked out the window. "Who's with you?"

"Hitchhiker."

Bobby headed down the hall. When he returned a few minutes later, Phyllis was outside at his truck. She stood next to Jack and seemed to be minding him. She brushed something away from his pants.

"Aw, shit," Bobby muttered.

Phyllis and Jack turned toward him when he exited. He didn't bother asking what happened and headed toward the gas pump.

"He fell," Phyllis said, "trying to get the walker out of the back."

"That so?" Bobby unscrewed the gas cap.

"Yeah, moron," Jack said. "I fell. Going to laugh?"

Phyllis furrowed her brow. "Why would he do that?"

"I wouldn't." Bobby jammed the nozzle into the

164

truck's gas tank. "Making fun of the disabled is something he would do."

"But you didn't get my walker out."

Bobby leaned his arms on the edge of the truck. He met his father's challenging gaze. "What was it you said, Jack? Any man that can't help himself. Did I get that right?"

His father scowled before turning and clattering the walker toward the store. Phyllis walked next to him and asked about his safety.

Bobby squeezed the handle, and the gas pump ticked as the fuel started.

***

"What's with the dog?" Jack asked.

They were northbound on Highway 25 again. His father had seemingly gotten over his fall.

"Everything is worth something," Bobby said.

Jack rolled his eyes. "I'm riding with the goddamned Buddha."

"What would you have done if the stroke hadn't happened?"

"Changing the subject are you?"

"Answer the question," Bobby said. "Were you going to do the whole forty?"

"I did twenty-two. You don't think I'm stand-up enough for the whole bit?"

Bobby shrugged. "I figured you would have ended it."

"You think I'm a pussy?"

"You talked pretty tough when I was a kid. Like how you'd never go in. Like how you'd never let them take you alive."

Jack lowered his head. "I tried. Just didn't work out

that way."

The sounds of the road overwhelmed the cab then—
the insistent hum of rubber against asphalt, the rumble of
the engine, and the little squeaks and groans of protesting
metal.

After ten miles, Jack looked up from his thoughts.
"Why'd we take this route?"

Bobby rested his left wrist on top of the steering wheel
and put his right arm along the back of the bench seat. He
didn't touch his father, though. His thumb hooked the top
of the seat and his fingers drummed along its back. "I
never take the interstate. Too many troopers looking to
make their quota."

"If you woulda gone through Wilbur and up through
Coulee Dam, it woulda saved more than an hour."

"Ever notice how many cops are in Coulee Dam?"

"Been a while."

"There's more than a few of them," Bobby said. "My
theory is the dam is some sort of strategic target. Traffic
funnels into that town, right by the dam, right by a line of
cops, then goes out. Doesn't matter which way. So, I
think an ounce of prevention is worth it."

Jack looked out the back window. "A lot of prevention
for delivering a dog."

"You just spent two decades in the can. Sit back and
enjoy the ride."

"How can I do that when you're driving the speed
limit?"

*   *   *

"Need to stop?" Bobby asked.

They were approaching the town of Republic.

"Nah," Jack said. "I'm good."

Neither man had spoken for the past half hour. Both were content to let the road work its magic. For Bobby, that was the solitude. There were moments while driving that he'd look around and let his imagination run wild. Out here where no other humans currently were, Bobby could think he was a man on some sort of futuristic quest. Sort of like Mel Gibson in the Mad Max movies but with a GMC 4x4 instead of a badass Ford Falcon.

He couldn't imagine that today, though, because Max didn't have his father in the car with him. What a mess that movie would have been. Probably still would have been better than that bloated remake with Tom Hardy.

"If we don't stop here," Bobby said, "we're not stopping until we get over the pass."

"I said I'm good."

"All right."

Jack turned to him. "What's got you so worried about my prostate all of a sudden?"

Bobby's face pinched. "Nothing. I was just being nice."

"Well, if you're being nice, I'm hungry."

"You said you ate before."

"I did."

"Good because we're not stopping for food."

"But you drive like time isn't important."

Bobby shook his head. "My time is important."

"What about mine?"

"If it was, you probably should have made different choices."

Jack squinted. "You're a sumbitch."

"Like father, like son."

"I know what you're doing," Jack said. "What you're delivering."

"Yeah?"

"Drugs."

"Is that right?" Bobby said. He didn't bother looking at his father.

"They're probably under the dog's platform. I'm not stupid, you know."

"Whatever you say."

"Am I right?"

Bobby shrugged. "No idea."

"You've never checked?"

"Why would I? I get paid to drive from one point to another and not get stopped along the way."

Jack leaned his head back. "You think those drugs are for the beaners?"

"Excuse me?"

"The ones who work the fields. Or did that change while I was away?"

"Stop talking."

Jack twisted in his seat to look out the rear window. "Maybe it's for the Canucks." His face scrunched. "Although that doesn't seem like a lot of drugs. How much do you think they got under that dog?"

"No idea."

"What if it's stolen jewels?" Jack smiled that lopsided grin of his. "How crazy would that be? You smuggling hot rocks into Canada. Hardy Fry did that kind of shit all the time—hauling contraband in and out of the Great White North."

"Sure, he did."

"Why do you say it like that?"

"Because I think half the shit Hardy Fry did was lies."

"That's not true."

"The other half is stuff people want to believe is true."

Jack sneered at his son. "What happened to you?"

"You did."

They pulled into the small town of Tonasket. Omak was thirty minutes to the south, while the Canadian Border was twenty minutes to the north. Bobby entered the downtown area and found a parking spot on Third Avenue.

"What are we doing?" Jack asked. His head swiveled about.

"Grabbing some lunch."

"Don't you wanna get rid of the mutt first?"

Bobby slid from the cab and walked over to the passenger side. He grabbed the walker from the truck bed. Jack's door squeaked open, and he stepped unsteadily down.

"Here." Bobby set the walker in front of this father.

"Look at you, being all considerate now."

"C'mon. Get out of the way." Bobby slammed the passenger door.

Jack eyed the dog as it silently watched him. "Godzilla never barks."

"Let's go."

Bobby walked around the corner to Whitcomb Avenue and The Iron Grill. Large windows ran along the face of the one-story brown brick building. He waited at the door as his father slowly clanked and dragged his way.

They found a table near the front. A news program silently ran on the television above the bar. Some country-western music softly played in the background.

When a server approached, she carried two glasses of iced water and two paper menus. "Get you boys something other than water?"

"I'm good," Bobby said. He accepted one of the

menus.

"Coffee," his father said. "Black."

Jack's head bobbed in time with the music as they studied the menus. "This is a good one." He looked up from the paper he held. "You don't like it?"

"What are you having?"

"Just got the menu. You already know?"

He pushed his chair back. "When she gets back, order me the house burger."

"Where you going?"

"The head." Bobby walked toward the rear of the restaurant. He glanced over his shoulder to ensure Jack wasn't watching, then slipped out the back door.

Bobby climbed into his truck, fired it up, and drove several blocks to a warehouse on North Locust Way. It was a small structure with flaking paint and cracked windows. It had two doors—a man-sized one and another for vehicles. He spun the steering wheel and turned into the street. He dropped the transmission into Reverse and backed toward the building. The large door rolled up.

After the truck entered the bay, a stocky Hispanic man Bobby knew as Hector yanked down on the chain and closed the door. The sunlight was replaced by fluorescent bulbs.

Bobby slipped out of the truck.

Hector ambled over. He had short black hair and distrusting eyes. He wore dirty denim overalls and wiped his hands on a filthy rag. "How was the drive?"

"The same."

Two white men in their early twenties came out of a backroom—Bobby never bothered to learn their names and didn't dare ask. Both wore similar overalls as Hector's. They popped the GMC's tailgate; it squeaked just before it thunked into position. One of the men opened the crate, and the Rottweiler jumped down.

"How'd Suzie do?" Hector asked.

"Like usual."

Hector stood on his tiptoes and craned his neck to investigate the crate. Bobby knew what he was looking for. "Phyllis called."

"I figured."

The two younger men unhooked the straps holding the crate in place.

Hector dropped to his usual height. Additional suspicion filled eyes. "She said you picked up a hitchhiker."

"That's what I told her."

"So it wasn't?"

Bobby shook his head. "He's my father."

"Was it take-your-pops-to-work day?"

"Something like that."

One of the younger men walked out the rear door with the dog. The other dragged the crate from the truck bed. It clunked to the ground.

"Where's your father now?"

"The Iron Grill."

Hector frowned. "You know I'm going to have to report it."

Bobby nodded. "Tell them he just got out of Walla Walla."

"You going soft?"

"No."

"Does he know what you were delivering?"

Bobby forced a smile. "I don't even know what I'm delivering."

Hector didn't return the gesture.

"I told him I was delivering the dog."

The man with the crate dragged it into the corner. He

then went back into the little room.

Hector rubbed his mouth. "You're a good driver, Bobby. You normally don't take risks."

"He's an old man. This wasn't a risk."

"You're sure you weren't followed?"

"I checked repeatedly. Why do you think I stopped to see Phyllis? I wanted you to know."

The back door to the warehouse opened and the second man entered with the dog. The Rottweiler roamed freely around. Something was in the man's gloved hand as he went toward the restroom.

Hector inhaled deeply. "I'm still gonna have to call. Stay at the grill until I come see you."

***

Bobby finally put it together after the one and only time the Rottweiler crapped in the crate. Until then, Bobby suspected but couldn't pin it down. He knew something was amiss when he was asked to deliver a second dog—another Rottweiler.

Like the first, that animal never barked—it just stared at him.

Bobby wasn't a dog person, but it seemed possible that it was the same Rottweiler. It had similar coloring and the same thick head. Yet, how could he be sure? It's not like he spent a lot of time with the dogs, and it wasn't like he could take them out and play. So, he studied the crate and noticed a nick on the black platform—an S-shaped scratch near the front.

The third delivery confirmed the crate had returned to Spokane. It was the S-shaped mark that did it. In Bobby's mind, that meant the Rottweiler inside was likely the same, too. Why did the same quiet dog need to be trekked across Eastern Washington three times?

On that delivery, Bobby braved the comment, "She's a good dog."

Hector eyed him. "Yeah. Suzie's a good girl."

The deliveries weren't on any set schedule. Bobby would receive a call, and he'd meet to pick up the dog. It was always at the same spot, though—a dumpy warehouse in Spokane Valley, much like the destination in Tonasket.

It was during the sixth delivery that the dog shit in the crate. The process went much the same as today. One man walked Suzie outside while the other dragged the crate from the truck bed. Bobby always thought it strange that the man returning from outdoors still wore the blue glove and headed straight for the restroom. He didn't have the guts to ask why.

Bobby was about to leave after the sixth delivery, but Hector insisted he stay and watch. The second man yanked the black platform from the crate. He then slipped on a blue latex glove. Hector didn't watch the other man dig through the dog's feces. Instead, he studied Bobby.

While the younger man smushed his fingers through the dog's mess, Bobby kept his expression flat. He didn't know what the man searched for, but Bobby now knew for certain he wasn't delivering drugs or guns to Tonasket. That's what he had initially suspected. Until that moment, Bobby thought something was hidden under the platform and they waited for him to leave before removing it. The veil of his naivety was removed as the younger man rubbed his fingers together as if sifting for something inside the feces. When the man abruptly stood, he glanced at Hector and nodded before heading for the restroom.

Hector patted Bobby on the back and told him he

could go. Nothing was ever said about what was witnessed.

Bobby wasn't ignorant of what would happen next. Whatever was inside the dog would be secreted into Canada somehow. Perhaps it would be fed to Suzie again, and she'd be taken across the border.

But what kind of information needed to be delivered that way? Why couldn't it simply be sent via computer or uploaded into the cloud? Bobby wasn't a technical guy, but he understood some of the notions. What he was doing with Hector seemed like an old-fashioned way of delivering intelligence.

Bobby had watched enough spy movies to understand the concepts of concealment. What was so important to be transported this way? Could it have been something from Fairchild Air Force Base? Was it a terrorist network communicating in ways that couldn't be intercepted by satellite or other computers?

In the end, Bobby didn't care. It paid well, and he got to drive.

That's what mattered.

***

When Bobby entered the restaurant, Jack put down his fork. He wiped his hands and watched his son settle into his chair.

"That must've been some dump," Jack said.

"You have no idea."

Bobby pushed his baseball hat back on his head before lifting his burger. It was still warm. He hadn't been gone that long. He bit into it.

"You just came in the front door," Jack said. "Did you think I wouldn't notice?"

Bobby continued to chew.

Jack lifted a French fry and studied it. "Let me guess. We were never going to Omak."

When Bobby didn't respond, Jack asked, "Something go wrong?"

"You did," Bobby said through a mouthful.

"Me? What'd I do?"

"You came along."

"How did they know I was even with you? You dropped me here then went and did your business." Jack's shoulders hunched, and he glanced around the restaurant. "Is one of their men in here?"

"No." Bobby bit into his burger again.

Jack crossed his arms. "What's this all about?"

"I told you not to come."

"Big deal if you brought someone."

"It is a big deal, Jack." Bobby dropped his burger back to the plate. "They don't know you."

"People know me. Back in the day, Transmission Jack meant something."

"Not anymore."

"Let them ask around. I still got a good reputation."

"Twenty-two years is a long time to forget."

"People never forgot Hardy," Jack said. "They won't forget me."

Bobby's lip curled. "He never went to prison."

Jack rubbed a shaky hand over his lips. "I didn't want that."

"You keep saying that."

"It's true." Jack shook his head. "I didn't hit that cop just to hit him."

"Then why do it?"

"If you would have come and visited, I would have told you."

"Tell me now."

Jack leaned in and lowered his voice. He glanced around a couple of times before speaking. "The job had gone sour." He looked around once more. "I knew I wasn't getting away. The others did, but the cops had me. So I did what I thought was right."

"You killed a cop."

"I tried to kill myself." Jack seemed embarrassed by his admission. He glanced around yet again and lowered his voice further. "The cop was collateral damage. I hit his car. Caught him right behind the support panel."

Bobby knew this from the reports he'd read as a teenager, but he let his father tell him. Jack never shared any of this with Bobby before going to prison.

"When I did it," Jack said, "I didn't think about you. There was no time. Afterward, sure. I thought a lot about you, then. I always figured you'd go live with your mother."

"She left, remember? Besides, you taught me never go after a woman who leaves."

Jack picked up another French fry to study. Bobby didn't know what his father found so fascinating with them. "So you did pay attention to something?"

The door to the Iron Grill opened, and Hector walked in. He paused long enough to let his eyes adjust to the lower light, then headed toward Bobby.

"You know this greaser?" Jack whispered.

Hector stopped and bent toward Bobby's ear. "They like you, but this is a warning. You only get one. Understand?"

Bobby nodded.

"If you ever bring anyone again—" Hector didn't finish the threat.

"I understand."

Hector never bothered looking at Jack before leaving. Jack chuckled. "Like he's so tough."

"Stop talking." Bobby waved at the server.

***

Against his better judgment, Bobby took the quicker way back to Spokane. Hector's threat left him jittery, and he'd spent enough time with his father. He just wanted to get home. Bobby drove south through Omak, then funneled through the small city of Coulee Dam. They were on the outskirts of town when blue and red lights flashed in his rearview mirror.

"Shit," Bobby muttered.

Jack looked over his shoulder. He chuckled. "Looks like you were right about this place."

Bobby pulled to the side of the road, and a patrol car zoomed past him.

Jack's chuckle faded. "Lucky sumbitch."

A mile up the road, they came to a collision. Several patrol cars blocked their path, and a uniformed officer waved for Bobby to take a detour.

"Lucky sumbitch," Jack muttered again.

***

Jack cocked his head. "You going to make googly eyes at her when we get home?"

"What?" Bobby asked.

"Shawna. When we get home, are you going to do that stupid look?" Jack bulged his eyes. "You know the one you did this morning?"

Bobby's face pinched. "No."

"Good because that look isn't gonna help you see her

lady parts. You got a big enough hill to climb with your regular face."

"Christ," Bobby muttered. "Stop talking."

They traveled a couple of miles in silence. Jack drummed his fingers on the passenger door handle. The rhythmic noise bothered Bobby.

"Give it a rest," he said.

Jack faced him. "Can I give you some advice?"

"No."

"Well, I'm going to anyway."

Bobby lifted a hand in frustration. "Of course, you are."

"This is important. Pay attention."

"Whatever."

Jack leaned closer to him. "Women are like macaroni and cheese at a Chinese buffet."

Bobby pulled away. His attention bounced from the road ahead to his father. "Are you for real?"

"What's the problem? I didn't say gook."

"Aw fuck, Jack!" He smacked the steering wheel. "You can't say stuff like that."

"Don't get your panties in a bunch. I should have told you this when you were younger."

"I'm good," Bobby said. "Leave me be."

"No, you're not good. I saw you looking at her. So as I was saying—that mac and cheese might look good and all, but you can't trust it. What's it doing there?"

Bobby squinted. "What?"

"What do you mean *what*? They still got them buffets, don't they? That didn't change while I was inside, did it?"

"No, and they're called Asian buffets now."

"Whatever, but you know what I'm talking about. That macaroni and cheese might look tasty, maybe even smell that way, but it's highly suspect. Think about that while you're making them googly eyes."

"Enough, Jack, enough."

His father harrumphed. "That's the problem with you, moron. I got all this good advice, and you think you're too smart to take it."

***

When Bobby pulled to a stop in front of Jack's home, he slipped the truck into Park. He caught a glimpse of himself in the rearview mirror and retightened the brim of his baseball hat.

"Here she comes," Jack said.

Shawna walked casually down the sidewalk.

Jack turned to Bobby. "Let me put a good word in for you."

"No." Bobby watched Shawna approach.

"Don't make that face, moron. I already told you about that."

"For the love of God," Bobby said. He slipped out of the truck and hustled around to the other side.

Shawna popped open Jack's door. It swung wide with a metallic groan.

Bobby grabbed the walker from the truck bed and put it next to Shawna. "We made it back in time."

"I see that," she said.

Jack slipped an arm around Shawna's shoulder as he slid from the truck's bench seat. He eyed Bobby. "Last chance."

"No," Bobby snapped. His brow furrowed as he grabbed his father's free arm. "Not a damn word."

"Whatever you say."

Shawna looked between the two men as they helped

Jack to his walker. "What's going on?"

"My son doesn't believe me," Jack said.

"What doesn't he believe?" she asked.

"That you saw my wanger."

Bobby blanched as he now stared directly into Shawna's face.

She lifted an eyebrow before turning slowly to Jack. "Your wanger?"

"I'm trying to be polite. If you want, I can call it my—"

"Jack!" Bobby blurted.

Shawna stared at Bobby. "Is this what you two talked about today?" She asked the question like a high school librarian scolding him for an overdue book. Bobby couldn't explain why he liked it.

He smiled nervously. "He's messing around."

"Don't let him fool you," Jack said with that goofy lopsided grin. "All day long. It was the only thing he talked about—you and my wanger."

Shawna smirked. "Is that so?"

"Oh, yeah." Jack nodded. "I tried to get him to stop, but he kept on going. I even told him you probably saw a lot of wangers."

"Christ," Bobby whispered.

"A lot of wangers?" Shawna's eyes widened with disbelief.

Jack looked innocently at her. "I mean because of your job and all."

"And all?" she repeated.

"That's right." Jack waved a hand up and down her length. "You're a pretty girl. You've probably had more than your fair share of chances."

Shawna faced Bobby. He turned his palms upward in a helpless gesture.

"The kid didn't want to hear none of that."

"Neither do I." Shawna grabbed Jack's elbow and helped him to the sidewalk. When they were on solid ground, she looked back and studied Bobby. "This is what you talked about?"

He felt uncomfortable under her gaze, yet he sort of enjoyed the feeling.

"Googly eyes," Jack muttered.

Bobby scowled at his father. "Enough."

"When are you gonna be back?" Shawna asked.

"Tomorrow?" Bobby's eyes widened with hope. "I can be back early if you want. Or I can follow you inside now if that's better."

"No hurry," she said. His eagerness melted her interest. She held onto Jack's arm. "C'mon, let's go."

Bobby unconsciously leaned forward. He needed to say something—*anything*—before she left. It seemed as if they almost established a connection.

"Mac and cheese," Jack said. "How many times do I have to tell you?"

Shawna cocked her head, and Bobby looked away.

Jack frowned. "The moron'll eat anything from a Chinese buffet."

"Never the mac and cheese," Shawna scolded.

Bobby patted his chest. "I don't. I haven't."

Her disapproving look wasn't so satisfying right now.

Jack jerked a thumb toward Shawna. "Want me to fill her in?"

"What am I missing?" she asked.

"Nothing," Bobby said. "Ignore him." He headed for the driver's side of the truck. "I'll see you tomorrow."

"How about I tell her how you drive?"

"Stop talking, Jack."

"Like an old woman," his father said. "That's how. I

walk faster than he drives."

The door screeched as Bobby yanked it open. He climbed inside and gunned the engine.

Jack slowly clanked away with Shawna at his hip. Bobby watched them go. For a guy as harmless as a toothless Chihuahua, the old man sure gave him a rough day.

Bobby dropped the truck into gear, stomped the gas pedal, and roared from the neighborhood.

Epilogue for a Living Legend

Detective James Morgan rested the back of his head against the seat of his Dodge Charger. He was awake, but his eyelids drooped. He viewed the world through heavy lashes. Detective Nayla Senai sat in the passenger seat. Her head was bent over her phone. A thumb occasionally swiped across the screen.

The crowd gathered at The Red Apple Nursing Home had grown over the afternoon. Morgan tried to count the attendees at one point but quit at forty-three. There was too much movement, and these people were joyful. Signs and banners bounced in the air as the crowd sang and swayed. A woman in a loose-fitting dress twirled along the sidewalk.

These people had gathered to celebrate the life of Hardy Fry—a legendary getaway driver. In the eyes of law enforcement, he was a career criminal. Yet the only conviction that ever stuck to the man was a drunk in public almost forty years ago. He'd hardly be more of a criminal than most college students by his court record.

The freak show in the parking lot irked Morgan. Retired Detective Alan Tannenhill had commented earlier that something was wrong with society when it celebrated the life of a criminal. What did it say when they glorified his death?

Morgan lazily turned his head to Senai. "What're you doing?"

"Working."

"Looks like you're twittering."

She looked up. "What's that?"

"Talking on the internet."

Senai rolled her eyes. "It's amazing they haven't put you in the Law Enforcement Museum yet."

"They're gonna give me my own wing."

"They'll need it for your ego."

He chuckled and turned his attention back to the crowd. "What're they singing?"

"I don't know. They've been doing it for hours. You'd think some of them would get tired and go home."

"Two-Pistols Pauly and Hammerhead Hendrick did." The old geezers had shuffled off over an hour ago.

Senai glanced around. "The Tannenhills are gone."

Morgan hadn't seen the couple leave. Alan Tannenhill and his wife had wanted to be around to see Hardy fade away. Morgan grunted. "This is a bust."

"You're just figuring that out?"

"I guess I got more patience than you."

"Old people normally do." Senai dropped her gaze back to the phone. "We sat here all afternoon, and no one good showed up."

"Someone might have."

"But they didn't."

Morgan put his hands on the steering wheel and pulled himself into an upright position. "Maybe Hardy will die."

She eyed him. "Everyone does sooner or later."

He waved a dismissive hand. He was about to argue but decided against it. What was the point? Driving out to the nursing home felt like an inspired decision several hours ago. Now it seemed as if he had wasted an afternoon. "Let's call it a day."

Senai sighed with great relief. "Finally."

Morgan reached for the ignition key but hesitated. "Look at those assholes."

"Who?"

"There. The bus."

Senai squinted as she searched ahead. "Is that Roy?"

"With those dead beats."

Three white men exited a stopped Spokane Transit Authority bus. Along with Roy Utt were two shabbily dressed white men. The first had dark hair and wore a brown corduroy sport coat over a light blue T-shirt. His black jeans had a split alongside the right leg to the thigh. The second man wore a green baseball hat, a long-sleeved black T-shirt, and blue jeans frayed at the heels.

After the bus drove off, the three men crossed the street and walked into the parking lot.

Roy Utt draped his arms over the shoulders of the other men. He shuffled as the other two slowly walked. Roy wore only a single Converse tennis shoe. On his other foot was an exposed pink sock that had developed a hole in the big toe.

Morgan opened his car door.

"We're going to talk with them?" Senai asked.

"Stay here if you want, but I'm contacting someone today, so it doesn't feel like a total waste."

"But these guys—"

Morgan didn't wait for her protest. He climbed out, shut the door, and headed toward the men. Behind him, he heard Senai's door open.

The crowd sang a mangled version of The Bee-Gees "Stayin' Alive." The only words they got right were the repeated, "Ah, ah, ahs," followed by the song's title. They sang it over and over like a skipping record.

Morgan would love to smack the side of this crowd and reset the song.

The dark-haired man with Roy noticed Morgan approaching. His eyes widened, and he muttered something to the brown-haired guy. The two stopped walking and ducked underneath Roy's outstretched arms. The junkie continued to shuffle along with his head bowed. His unsupported gait became sloppier with each step.

Morgan caught up to Roy and grabbed him by the arm. "Hold on there, buddy."

"Morgan?" he mumbled.

"Let's go see your friends."

Senai arrived at Morgan's shoulder. "Those two know you."

"I'm a popular guy."

Morgan spun Roy around, which caused the junkie to fall into the detective's arms. "Easy, pal."

The guy with the brown hair lifted a cell phone in front of his face like he was filming Morgan. The green trucker-style baseball hat sat cattywampus on his head and had its logo patch ripped off. The holes from the stitching were visible when Morgan got closer.

"Put the phone away, jackass," the detective said.

"I got a right," the brown-haired man said.

"You got a right to have my foot in your ass, Tom. Put it away."

Tom reluctantly lowered the cell phone.

"The fuck," the dark-haired man said. He smacked Tom's arm, then jerked a thumb at Morgan. "Don't let him bully you. Video his ass."

"You want my foot, too, Joe?"

The dark-haired man appeared offended. "What'd I do? He's the one with the camera."

Roy started to sway, and Morgan pulled him back toward him. "What're you three doing here?"

Tom started to speak, but his friend interrupted him.

"Listen, Herr Kommandant, we got a right to be here," Joe said. He put his hands on his hips, which pushed the corduroy jacket back. It revealed the light blue Britney Spears T-shirt—the one where she looked fourteen as she sat on her knees looking up at the camera. "You think you can take away our right to assemble peaceably?"

"Oh, that's nice," Tom said. "Peaceably."

"Thank you." Joe bowed slightly. "I'm expanding my vocabulary. You should try it sometime."

Tom rolled his eyes. "That coat is going to your head."

"You're just jealous." A breeze came across the lot and blew the flap of Joe's ripped jeans open to expose his bare leg. "I got style, and you don't."

"What is it with you two jagoffs?" Morgan asked. Roy swayed again, and Morgan tugged him closer. "Always with the Laurel and Hardy routine."

Tom and Joe looked at each other. They pointed fingers at one another and then shook their heads.

"Abbott and Costello maybe," said Tom.

"Yeah." Joe nodded. "Keenan and Kel, perhaps."

Tom frowned. "Who?"

"You know. *Good Burger*?" Joe shook his head. "I don't know why I hang out with you."

"Why didn't you say, Martin and Lewis? Or Hope and Crosby? We're doing a classic comedy riff, and you go with some guys from *Good Burger*. Wasn't that on Nickelodeon or something?"

"Keenan and Kel are from the nineties. They're considered classic." The breeze returned and whipped the flap of jeans open again. "Like me."

"Oh, you're classic all right," Tom said.

Morgan eyed Senai. "Why don't you take Roy over to the car? Let me talk to these two alone."

Senai shrugged. "Yeah, okay." She grabbed the junkie's other arm.

"Hold on," Joe said to Senai. He reached out to touch

her elbow, but she pulled back.

"No touching," the detective said.

Joe lifted his hands in mock surrender. "It's not like that." He glanced at Morgan, and then his gaze returned to Senai. "It's just that we'd prefer if you stayed." He looked at his friend. "Isn't that right?"

Tom nodded. "Yeah, for sure. Morgan's not our biggest fan." He turned to Morgan and nervously smiled. "Not that we don't like you."

Senai smirked. "Tell the man what he wants to know, and I'll stay."

Joe faced Morgan. "All right, fine. What is it you want?" As an afterthought, he added, "Detective."

Tom nodded approvingly. "Well played."

Morgan appraised the two men. "You guys holding?"

Both Joe and Tom reared back as if offended by the accusation.

"Are you implying drugs?" Joe said.

Tom touched his chest. "Do we look like the type to use illegal narcotics?"

Roy Utt held out his hand. "Hook a brother up."

Joe slapped the open palm. "Shut up, Roy." To Morgan, he said, "No, sir. Neither my associate nor I are holding illegal narcotics at this moment." He smiled proudly. "Now, out of our way, good man."

Morgan shoved Roy to Senai. "Take him to the car."

Both Joe and Tom held out their hands. "Wait!"

Senai pushed Roy back to Morgan.

Tom chuckled politely. "What my friend was trying to say is, how can we help you, Detective?"

"What are you three doing here?"

Tom waggled his phone.

"Does that even have service?" Morgan asked.

Joe clucked his tongue. "You don't need service to

make movies, Morgan. Don't you know anything?"

Morgan lifted an eyebrow. "I know how to knock your dick in the dirt."

Tom pointed over the detective's shoulder. "We came out here to make a documentary about Hardy Fry."

"And do what with it?" Morgan asked.

"Sell it to the Netflix," Joe said. "Those guys pay like millions for this stuff. We heard documentaries are the next big wave."

"Where'd you hear that?" Senai asked.

Joe shoved his hands into the pockets of the corduroy jacket. "We hear stuff. Don't let our current financial situation fool you. We get around town."

Tom motioned to Roy. "He was telling us how his sister subscribes to the channel and watches their shows all the time."

"But why Hardy?" Morgan asked.

"Because he's a living legend." Joe clapped his hands as if to emphasize each word. "Everyone knows about him. Look it." He lifted his chin toward the people dancing and singing in front of the nursing home. "There's your proof positive."

"A half a million people live in the county," Morgan said, "and maybe a hundred people showed up to see Hardy Fry out. You got a real blockbuster on your hands, hotshot."

Joe's smile melted. "I think you're shitting on our parade."

Tom leaned over to his friend and lowered his voice. "I don't think you're using that right."

Joe waved his hands even though they remained in the jacket pockets. He looked like a man flapping corduroy wings. "Jesus, Tom, don't you see what he's doing? He's stomping on our creativity. He doesn't want us to make this movie. He wants to keep the legend of Hardy Fry secret."

A groan erupted through the crowd, and the festivities stopped.

Joe and Tom both tried to look around Morgan.

A man holding an *Everyday is Fry Day* sign over his shoulder walked by. His head was down, and he muttered to himself.

"What happened?" Senai asked the man.

"He's dead," the man said.

"Hardy?" Tom asked.

"Who else?"

Joe angrily turned to Morgan. "Look what you did. You just cost us a million bucks. Each!"

Morgan laughed once. "Listen, dumb ass—"

"Video him." Joe smacked his friend's arm. "Do it."

"Yeah," Tom said, "I don't know."

"We could have gotten the movie made," Joe said. "You know it." He pointed at Morgan. "He knows it, too. That's why he stole our futures."

"I'm going back to the car," Senai said.

"Wait for me," Morgan said. He shoved Roy toward Joe and Tom. The dead beats caught their friend. "You boys ever get that movie made, you let me know. I'll buy tickets for the whole department. I'll even spring for popcorn."

"We will," Joe said. "Trust me."

Tom touched his friend's arm, but Joe yanked it away.

"You just wait and see. It's gonna get made if it's the last thing we do. Then who's gonna laugh?"

"Hold on," Tom said quietly.

Joe's face pinched. "What?"

Tom thumbed in Morgan's direction. "If we make the movie, he's gonna bring the whole department."

"The whole department?"

"That's what he said."

Joe's expression flattened, and he looked at Morgan. "Never mind what I said."

"Yeah," Tom said. "Never mind what he said."

"The project won't get off the ground." Joe chuckled nervously. "You know how it is, Morgan. Inadequate funding."

Each man hurriedly grabbed one of Roy's arms. The three of them shuffled out of the parking lot. After they walked around the corner, Morgan headed back to the car.

When he dropped into the driver's seat, Nayla asked, "Everything work out okay?"

"Uh-huh," Morgan said. He reached for the ignition key. "They just needed a lesson in the rules of Hollywood."

"Which you understand?"

"Of course." He turned the key, and the engine rumbled to life.

"Care to enlighten me?"

"Legends die." Morgan dropped the gear shift into Drive. "Not everybody wants to see that movie."

The tires chirped as the Charger roared from the parking lot.

Towed Away

A flatbed tow truck sat quietly in the middle of an activity maelstrom. Usually, it was a tertiary player in moments like this, but today the vehicle and its driver were the stars. They were in the vacant parking lot on the northwest corner of Mission Avenue and Hamilton Street. Two lines of yellow POLICE—DO NOT CROSS tape circled the small lot, marking outer and inner perimeters.

Spokane Police Detective Quinn Delaney slipped under the outer line to meet his partner, Marci Burkett. She wore a black pantsuit, a blue silk shirt, and black shoes. Her dark hair was cut in a punkish style—heavy on the bangs, short on the sides. It reminded Quinn of Joan Jett in her heyday.

Marci waved her notebook at the commotion surrounding them. "You believe this?"

The intersection was one of the busiest in Spokane, with eight lanes—twelve if the turn lanes were added. It sat in the shadow of Gonzaga University and was on the periphery of downtown. Hamilton Street funneled northsiders to and from Interstate 90. Vehicular traffic remained busy throughout the day, while pedestrians were usually sparse.

Today, however, clusters of college students gathered on the sidewalks at the edge of the crime scene. Many held their cell phones in the air and pointed them toward the tow truck. Several uniformed officers stood nearby to limit the looky-loos from getting too close.

Quinn shrugged. "School's in session."

"That's my point," Marci said. "Those baby lawyers

should be there, not here."

"Maybe they have online classes," Quinn murmured.

Marci rolled her eyes. "Oh, that's great. They're learning how to eat their young even more efficiently."

Quinn didn't feel like arguing. Not because he didn't enjoy verbally sparring with his partner—he did. It was that he didn't want to do it under the watchful eye of two dozen college students and their cell phones.

He turned to survey the lot. Years prior, it had been a car wash. At the end of its useful life, the structure was demolished. Since then, weekend entrepreneurs trespassed onto the lot to sell everything from Rottweiler puppies to sports-themed blankets to cheap sunglasses.

Hungry passersby would occasionally intrude onto the lot and eat takeout from the neighboring, drive-thru-only McDonald's. Quinn himself had done that after leaving a different crime scene some months ago.

The vacant lot's owners never complained about encroachment, and the city's code enforcement unit responded accordingly—it ignored the situation. They all might change their tune now, Quinn thought.

Members of the Spokane Police Department's traffic unit blocked the closest lanes on Mission and Hamilton. Red and blue emergency lights flashed from atop their patrol vehicles. Horns honked as commuters merged into single-file lanes.

"Ready?" Marci asked.

Quinn headed for the inner perimeter. An officer with a clipboard stood by the tape. His blue nametag read *Silva,* and the rookie was responsible for tracking who entered and left this area. Quinn ducked under the tape but didn't bother holding it for Marci. He had tried that once, and she punched him in the arm for it. He never did it again.

She bobbed under the yellow tape like a fighter slipping a punch.

"What do we know?" Quinn asked her.

"I just got here myself and only got a quick debrief from the sergeant." She motioned across the lot. "He's with some possible witnesses right now. Anyway, dispatch called the tow company, McDougan Tow Yard, who said the truck was signed out to one of their drivers—Brandon Rice. They ran him through NCIC. Petty entries from years ago, but no felonies."

Quinn raised an eyebrow. "Could he tow if he was a convicted felon?"

She shrugged. "I don't think so. Maybe. Doesn't matter, though, since he wasn't."

They approached the tow truck from the driver's side, studying the Harley Davidson strapped to its flatbed. On the side of the black, teardrop-shaped gas tank were airbrushed wisps of smoke around the word *Widowmaker*. They couldn't see what was on top of the tank.

"It couldn't be," Marci said. She hurriedly climbed onto the flatbed. She dusted herself off as she moved forward. "Whoever owns this bike is a Wasted Soul."

Quinn didn't need to climb up to know what she saw. He was familiar with the biker club's logo—a skull shrouded in smoke.

Marci turned and hollered. "Yo, Silva!" When she got the rookie's attention, she pointed at the motorcycle. "Run the plate, find the R.O., and then check their background. Got it?"

Quinn moved toward the cab. The driver's door was closed, but the window was rolled down. Blood spatter was visible on the front windshield. To see inside the truck's cab required climbing onto the side-step. Quinn squatted and examined the stainless-steel platform. It didn't appear as if any blood or other evidence was there.

Marci moved next to him as she tugged on a pair of blue latex gloves.

"Want the first look?" Quinn asked.

She ascended the step and peered through the window. Marci remained quiet for several moments. While she was up there, Quinn pulled a pair of latex gloves from the pocket of his suit jacket and slipped them on.

Marci hopped down. "You'll like this one."

Quinn stepped up and was careful where he put his hands. He wanted to ensure he didn't smudge possible fingerprints, so he held onto the side mirror's support bar.

Blood and brain matter smeared the inside of the windshield. A man slumped to the right; his weight was caught by the seatbelt. The skull's left side was blown away and spread about the cab. Tiny slivers of bone were stuck in the window visor.

Quinn imagined the shooter climbing onto the side-step to confront Brandon. The detective leaned back and extended his hand like an imaginary gun. The driver would have had nowhere to go because he was in his seatbelt.

He dropped his thumb. *Blam!*

"That's sick!" a young woman hollered.

Quinn looked over his shoulder to the group of onlookers with their phones raised in the air. He lowered his arm and reconsidered the dead man.

It was likely the shooter kept the gun tight to the victim so a potential witness couldn't see what was occurring. That probably meant it was a quick movement—the shooter brought the gun from its hiding place into the cab, where it was fired. If it was slow, Brandon might have fought it off or a witness might have seen it.

Quinn stepped off the platform. Behind the crowd of onlookers, a boxy white truck pulled to the curb. The Spokane County Forensics Unit had arrived.

"Pretty brazen," Marci said, "killing someone on this stage."

"People stop here during the day," Quinn said. "Even I've had lunch here before. A guy walking up to a parked vehicle wouldn't seem too out of the ordinary."

"Somebody had to notice this guy getting shot in the head." she said, looking over the crowd. "Someone had to hear it, at least."

"The cab's window is eight feet off the ground." Quinn looked up to the cab. "Seems like no one noticed it until there was blood."

"The driver probably knew his killer, don't you think?" Marci motioned toward the window. "It's rolled down."

Quinn considered Rice letting a stranger get close. "If the driver didn't know the shooter, he didn't fear them. Maybe a woman? An older man? Who gets you to drop your guard?"

"No one." Marci glanced back at the gaggle of college students. "You think one of them could have done it?"

Quinn shook his head. "Unlikely. I can't see them getting their hands dirty for this."

Officer Silva walked over. He ripped a piece of paper from his notepad and handed it to Marci. "The Harley's registered owner is Wyatt Schulte. He's got a history of assault. Some felonies. That's his address."

Marci waved the paper. "We might have caught a break. It's not the clubhouse."

Quinn was happy to hear that. He wouldn't have wanted to contact a member of the Wasted Souls at their local headquarters. The biker gang wasn't known for its hospitality, especially toward cops.

Marci asked Silva, "Any luck with the witnesses?"

The rookie pointed to the opposite side of the vacant lot where two adult women huddled with the sergeant. "There's a mother and her daughter who think they saw someone talking with the tow truck driver, but they can't be sure if it was a man or a woman."

Marci frowned. "That's helpful."

A semi-truck hauling cows drove southbound on Hamilton. Its engine roared and drowned out their conversation. The three waited until it passed.

"What about video?" Marci asked. "One of the businesses around here must have some. McDonald's, the dry cleaner, the gas station." She flicked her hand toward each as she listed them.

Silva shrugged. "The sergeant tasked some of the others to check into that. I'm on the log."

Quinn and Marci nodded their thanks, then moved beyond the last line of caution tape.

Geri Utley stepped out of the forensic unit's truck. She led the team and had worked many scenes with the two detectives. Geri smiled as she tucked her long, blond hair underneath a baseball cap. "Look who it is," she said. "Riggs and Murtaugh."

"Which one was Mel Gibson?" Quinn asked.

Marci tsked. "Ignore him. He knows. He just doesn't like being called Murtaugh."

"I was SWAT," Quinn said. "I should be Riggs."

"If you were partnered with Nash, maybe." Marci tapped her sternum. "But I'm clearly the Riggs in this relationship."

Geri smiled. "Are the two of you ready?" She grabbed a camera from the back of the truck. "Let's go see what we're dealing with."

For the next ninety minutes, Quinn and Marci stood by as Geri and the forensic team methodically processed the body and the tow truck's cab. First the team erected a large screen to limit the views of bystanders. This elicited loud groans and calls of derision from the assembled crowd of students.

Geri photographed each step her investigators made. They collected blood and tissue samples from the surfaces of the cab, found different colored hairs embedded in the cloth seats, and eventually pulled a slug from the vehicle's arm rest near the passenger door.

The forensic team didn't process the body while it was in the cab, though. The limited access and potential exposure to blood and other body tissue made it difficult.

When two men from the medical examiner's transport team arrived, they removed the body and placed it on a gurney. Quinn emptied the victim's pockets and Geri photographed the items. Then he deposited the various pieces into a clear plastic bag Marci held.

The medical examiner's men shoved the gurney into a hearse, and the body was whisked away.

Marci handed the plastic bag to Quinn. Inside were a wallet, a set of personal car keys, a cell phone, and thirty-two cents.

He removed the wallet and opened it. "It's confirmed. The driver was Brandon Rice."

Marci snagged the bag back from Quinn and removed the phone. She activated it. "The last call was from someone named Nadine. Looks like it came through roughly thirty minutes prior to the report of homicide."

"Could be the wife," Quinn suggested.

"Could be a girlfriend," Marci countered.

Geri shrugged. "If we're playing that game, why

couldn't it be his sister?"

Marci called the number, and it went directly to voicemail.

"You've reached Nadine. You know what to do."

The phone beeped, and Marci hung up. "Nadine. No last name." She tossed the phone back into the plastic bag and looked at Quinn. "Who do you want to talk with first?"

***

"We called him Sticky," Callum McDougan said. "As in the rice."

Quinn nodded. "I got it. What can you tell us about Brandon?"

They were in the office of McDougan's Tow Yard, which sat at the corner of Second and Perry. The dirty room smelled of oil and perspiration. A calendar featuring a cherry red Chevy Nova hung on the wall behind McDougan. Next to it was a Playboy calendar from 1974 with a chesty blonde arching her back. A classic rock station played through a blinking clock radio which sat on the metal credenza. The Lynyrd Skynyrd song faded and was replaced by a Banner Fuel commercial.

McDougan wore a faded blue T-shirt with the Mopar logo. His swivel chair squeaked as he leaned forward. He rested his hairy forearms along the edge of his desk. "I'm not sure how much I should say."

Quinn glanced at Marci. They both sat in torn pleather chairs. Her gaze remained firmly on McDougan, and she seemed unfazed by the man's statement. Quinn turned back to the tow yard owner. "Why won't you talk with us?"

"It's not that I won't," McDougan said. He grabbed a pen and bounced the end of it against the desk. "It's just maybe I should consult with my lawyer first."

Quinn pinned him with a practiced glare. "Were you involved in the murder of Brandon Rice?"

McDougan's brow furrowed. "Why'n the fuck would you say that?"

Quinn shrugged. "You're not talking to us."

"It's because I got a business." McDougan tossed the pen onto his desk. "Sticky was my agent."

"Your agent?" Quinn wondered what kind of business McDougan ran that needed an agent.

"It's a legal term." McDougan briefly eyed Marci before returning to Quinn. "Means he was my employee."

It was going to be one of those conversations, Quinn thought. He inhaled deeply to calm himself. When he paused, Marci jumped in.

"You got a contract with the city, right?" She motioned a hand around the small office. "To tow evidentiary vehicles and whatnot?"

McDougan's lips briefly pursed. "What's that got to do with anything?"

"You're not exactly forthcoming." She lightly kicked the back of the metal desk, and the gong reverberated through the office. "And the tow list is maintained at the chief's pleasure. All it takes is one call from us—"

McDougan held up a hand to interrupt her. "Hold on there, sweet cheeks."

Her expression soured. "It's Detective Burkett."

McDougan ignored her. "You got no right to cut my access to those tows."

"Then you better get with the truth," Marci jerked her thumb toward the door, "or we'll walk out of here and into the chief's office."

McDougan sneered at her. When she smiled, he eyed Quinn. "I like you better."

"Then tell us about Brandon Rice," Quinn said.

Marci dropped back into her chair and crossed her arms.

McDougan mimicked her motion; he flopped back in his chair and folded his arms over his barrel chest. "It's just Sticky might or might not have illegally seized that bike."

Quinn raised an eyebrow. "Might have?"

"Might not have," McDougan said quickly. "I don't know."

Quinn nodded, following the line of plausible deniability. "Where'd he get the motorcycle?"

"That's the issue. Your dispatcher said Sticky had a bike on the flatbed. I don't know nothing about that."

"You didn't dispatch him?" Marci asked.

McDougan's sneer returned. "Lady, what part of 'I don't know nothing about that' did you misunderstand?"

Marci faced her partner. "Let's go talk to the chief."

Quinn lifted a hand as a signal for her to wait. "You're running out of chances, McDougan."

McDougan pointed a thick finger at Marci. "Your partner has it out for me."

"Just tell us what you know," Quinn said, "and we'll leave you to your business."

McDougan briefly pursed his lips. "The last call Sticky had was for a broken-down BMW on the Sunset Highway. He delivered it to the customer's requested repair shop up on the north side. After that, he had some downtime."

Quinn nodded. "What did he normally do during time like that?"

"He usually came back here and worked on his wife's

car." McDougan motioned toward a window that overlooked the yard. "Nadine's got a clunker out there he's limping along. If they knew how to manage their money, they'd be dangerous. That woman has him wrapped around her finger. Ol' Sticky should show some backbone and put his foot down."

"If he didn't come back to the shop?" Quinn asked.

"He'd park the tow rig where he was and wait for the next call," McDougan said. "I didn't want him burning gas, what with inflation and all."

"So he went into a black hole today," Marci said, "and came out with a bike."

McDougan spread his hands wide. "That's what it looks like, sweet cheeks. What more can I say?"

***

The front door opened and revealed a large man in his early forties. His Black Label Society T-shirt was torn, and his faded blue jeans were frayed at the heels. His work boots were scuffed and untied. He had the thickness a man gets from lifting weights without ever paying attention to his diet. His gut pushed out, and it turned his belt buckle downward. Tattoos lined his muscular arms, most of them a blueish ink likely earned in prison.

"Wyatt Schulte?" Quinn asked.

"What about it?" the man answered with a growl.

Schulte lived in the East Central neighborhood, near Liberty Park. The Craftsman-style house had a small porch and a broken swing. An older, green Jeep Wagoneer was parked along the curb.

Quinn pulled his suit jacket to the side to reveal his gun and badge. "I'm Detective Delaney." He jerked his head toward Marci. "This is Detective Burkett. Are you the owner of a 2008 Harley-Davidson?" Quinn consulted his notebook and read the license plate number.

The big man folded his arms. "What about it?"

Quinn mimicked his stance. "Do you know where it's at?"

"By your question," Schulte said, "I'm supposing you do."

Quinn nodded. "We do."

Schulte frowned, and his shoulders slumped. "Guess you better come inside." He turned and walked in the house. The detectives followed.

There was no television in the front room, only a stereo system rack and a weight bench. Dumbbells sat clustered near the wall. Empty beer bottles were kept in an old box next to the door. It was a tidy place—a room that might remind a man of prison.

"Anyone in the house with you?" Quinn asked.

"Just me." Schulte dropped heavily onto the bench, then bent forward and rested his elbows on his knees. He eyed Marci. "Feel free to look around."

She walked toward the back of the house.

"About the bike," Quinn said.

"Stolen this morning," Shulte said. "I should prolly say thanks for finding it."

Quinn stayed in the middle of the room, giving him a line of sight to Marci. "Don't thank us yet. It was found at a murder scene."

Schulte put his hands on his knees and sat upright. "I didn't have nothing to do with whatever happened."

Of course not, Quinn thought. "Where was your bike when it was stolen?"

"Out front." He pointed at the window. "On the street."

"Was it locked?" Quinn asked, surprised.

Schulte's eyes flattened. "No. Only a dumbass would steal a bike that belongs to a Soul."

Quinn studied Schulte. "Are you the Widowmaker, or is that the bike's name?"

"Take your pick," Schulte said "Either works. 'Cept I didn't kill nobody today."

Marci returned to the room. "House is clear."

Schulte smirked. "Wouldn't have invited you to look if it wasn't."

Quinn asked, "Ever hear of Brandon Rice?"

The biker made a popping sound with his lips. "That's the dumbass responsible for this trouble, huh?"

"You know him?" Quinn asked.

"I know his old lady." Schulte smiled at Marci when he said it. "Is he the one who got himself killed?"

Marci asked, "Are you in a relationship with his wife?"

He grinned. "That's a polite way of putting it."

"You think Brandon knew about you two?" she asked.

Schulte chuckled. "Him stealing my bike sorta seals the deal he did, don't ya think?"

Quinn asked, "Do you have an alibi for earlier today?"

Schulte sobered. "I already told you; I didn't kill the man."

"That wasn't my question," Quinn said.

"Okay, Detective. How about I answer your question this way? I can alibi whatever time you say." Schulte stood and put a foot on the weight bench. "After the bike was stolen, I went to the clubhouse. Most of the brothers were there. I wanted to get them out looking for it."

Quinn frowned. Alibis given by members of the Wasted Souls were suspect. Even the truth became tainted by its proximity to their clubhouse. If Schulte was indeed involved in Rice's murder, it would be challenging to unpeel the fake alibi onion when it came time to prosecute. Quinn and Marci would need rock-solid proof.

"If your bike was stolen," Marci asked, "how'd you get to the clubhouse?"

Schulte pointed toward the window again. "That Jeep outside is my grocery-getter."

"Better question," Quinn asked. "Where were you when your bike was stolen? What were you doing?"

"Doing?" Schulte leered at Marci. "I was in the back of the house, doing Nadine."

"Spare me," she said.

"Not a chance, cop."

Quinn shook his head. "Mr. Schulte, would you be willing to come down to the station and take a GSR test?"

"Gunshot residue?" Schulte flicked his hand. "I'm not going anywhere, but if you wanna bring a test here, I'd do that. I didn't shoot that idiot, and I'm not going to jail for it."

***

Nadine Rice came to the front door with an unlit cigarette and a lighter in her right hand. Her gray flannel shirt hung open over a dull Soundgarden T-shirt. Her tight jeans flared out over bare feet. She leaned against the doorframe and affected a look of disinterest.

"Who are you?" she asked, more bored than curious.

Quinn and Marci had left Wyatt with a couple of patrol officers so he wouldn't have the opportunity to call Nadine.

The Rice home was in West Central. It was a dilapidated, two-story affair. The porch railing had failed and lay partially in the yard. There were no cars in the driveway and none out front.

Quinn opened his suit jacket to show his gun and badge. "Detective Delaney," he said. "This is my partner, Detective Burkett. Mind if we come in?"

"I do mind," Nadine said. She eyed Marci the way a pit bull might. "Does he always speak for you?"

Marci stared back but remained silent.

"The strong, quiet type, huh?" Nadine's gaze returned to Quinn. "I ain't seen the stupid sumbitch."

"Who?" Quinn asked.

"My brother. That's what this is about, right? Every so often, one of you types comes around looking for my brother, Raleigh." Her brow furrowed. "Raleigh Garmany."

Quinn glanced at Marci, who cocked her head in return. Almost everyone in the Spokane Police Department knew the man due to his lengthy criminal history. As far back as Quinn could remember, Raleigh had been in trouble for assaults, mischief, and robbery. The guy had both mental issues and substance abuse problems.

"Well, you can forget about it," Nadine said. "He hasn't been around here in forever. Not since my husband told him to get his worthless ass off our property."

"When was this?" Quinn asked.

"Last year." Nadine shook her head. "Or thereabouts. You think I would miss the fool, but he hasn't reached out in all that time to say he was sorry or nothing. As far as I'm concerned, my brother can stay gone."

"I'm sorry to break this to you," Quinn said, "but we're here about your husband."

"Brandon?" She poked the cigarette in between her lips. It bounced as she spoke. "What could he have done?"

"He died," Marci said.

It was a quick rip of the band-aid. Quinn doubted he would have broken the news that way, but Marci sensed something, and she jumped into the conversation. That's how interviews often went—back and forth, push and pull. Both detectives knew when to step back and let the other take lead. It wasn't about egos; it was about getting to the truth.

Nadine blinked several times. "He's dead?"

Marci cleared her throat. "Murdered."

"Oh, Christ." Nadine pulled the unlit cigarette from her mouth. "How?"

"Shot in the head." Marci held an imaginary gun to her temple.

Nadine grimaced. "Where did this happen?"

"In his tow truck," Marci said. "The corner of Mission and Hamilton."

Nadine covered her mouth. "You think Raleigh did it?"

"Why would you say that?" Marci asked. "You said you hadn't seen him in a while."

"Yeah, but Raleigh was upset at Brandon the last time. He said he'd get him back."

Marci made like she took a note. "What about Wyatt Schulte?"

"Who?" Nadine asked, trying for innocent and failing.

Marci smirked. "Please. We know."

Nadine's face hardened. "Why do you think he would have anything to do with Brandon's death?"

Marci sighed as if she hated explaining the obvious. "Because Brandon had Schulte's bike on the back of his tow truck. Souls aren't known for their sense of humor when it comes to their bikes."

Nadine shook her head. "Double Christ. Brandon

didn't."

"Oh, he did," Marci said. "He stole it while you two were in the middle of the hucklebuck. At least that's what Wyatt said."

Nadine frowned. "Think what you want, but what we do is not illegal." She stuck the cigarette back into her mouth and lit it.

Marci shifted her stance. "Do you think Wyatt capable of murder?"

Nadine exhaled two streams of smoke through her nose. "Oh hell. Wyatt didn't even know Brandon." She waved her hand about, and cigarette smoke trailed in the air. "To Wyatt, my husband was a figment of my imagination. Had he met Brandon, Wyatt wouldn't have worried none. That's like a wolf worrying about a house cat."

Marci put her hands on her hips. "You called your husband before his murder."

"I'm his wife." Nadine flicked ash from her cigarette. "I was seeing what he wanted for dinner. Ain't no crime in that."

"What did you decide?" Marci asked.

"That's a funny question." Nadine stepped onto the patio and both detectives took a half-step back. "You want my recipe for tuna casserole? I'll cut you a piece when it's done. It's cooking right now."

"Maybe next time," Marci said. "Just a few more questions. Where did you go after you left Wyatt's house?"

Nadine looked around the neighborhood. "I went grocery shopping. Needed some tuna and other groceries."

"Your car is at McDougan's auto shop," Quinn said. "How'd you get around?"

"I called an Uber," she said without faltering. "Haven't you ever been inconvenienced in your life?"

"How about you show us?" Marci asked.

Nadine's gaze settled on her. "Show you what?"

"Your cell phone." Marci motioned like she was dialing a number. "The Uber app. It should show when and where you were picked up."

Nadine's teeth clicked together. "It was Wyatt. He drove me."

"Why didn't you just say that?" Marci asked.

"Why do you think? I'm running around on my husband. It doesn't exactly look good, does it?"

Marci cocked her head. "Can you think of anyone who wanted to hurt your husband?"

"Besides my brother?"

"You've said. Anyone else?" Marci pressed.

Nadine clicked her tongue against the back of her teeth. "No one. Everybody loved Brandon. He was the kindest, most trusting man I ever met."

Marci raised her eyebrows.

"That didn't make him a good roll in the hay." Nadine flicked ash from the cigarette's end. "A woman still has her needs—you know?" Her gaze challenged Marci's. "That doesn't mean I killed my husband, and neither did Wyatt."

"You don't seem too upset by his death," Marci said.

Nadine's eyes narrowed. "Are you some sort of counselor, Detective? Do you suppose to know what's going on inside me right now?"

Marci shook her head slowly. "It was just an observation."

"You can keep those kinds of observations to yourself," Nadine snapped. "Is there anything else?"

***

Quinn tossed his notebook onto the desk before dropping into his chair. He tapped the space bar on his keyboard and called his computer to life. He grabbed his desk phone and called dispatch. It was answered on the first call.

"Annie," a woman said.

"It's Quinn. Do me a favor and put out an Attempt to Locate on Raleigh Garmany."

She clicked her tongue. "What'd he do now?"

Quinn cradled the phone between his ear and shoulder. "We'd like to talk to him about a homicide."

"He graduated to murder? Wow." There was clicking on a keyboard.

"Raleigh's only a person of interest," Quinn clarified. He didn't want an overeager patrol officer to engage Garmany as if the man was actually a suspect. Quinn still had work to do to move Garmany into that category.

"Person of interest," Annie said. "Okay, I'll let patrol know."

Quinn ended the call as Marci settled into her desk chair.

"So far," Quinn said, "the evidence isn't telling us much. It's going to be days, maybe a week, before we get the results back on the slug they pulled from the cab."

"If they can get anything from it," Marci added. "It looked pretty mangled."

"Then we've got to find the gun to match it to," Quinn said. "And we've got no decent witnesses to boot." He shook his head. "One of the busiest intersections in Spokane and nobody saw anything. How's that happen?"

"Patrol is still working on the video angle." Marci leaned back in her chair and put her feet up on the desk.

"I'm not optimistic we'll get anything useful."

"Me either," Quinn said. "How do you feel after interviewing Wyatt and Nadine?"

She crossed her arms. "I weep for our society."

Quinn smiled. "Beyond that. You think either of them could have done it?"

"Wyatt could have, but I doubt he did. Look at it this way. First, it was sloppy and in broad daylight. Second, he left his bike on the flatbed. Why? It points us right at him and the Souls. No way he would do it like that. The guy's a meatball, but he's not that dumb."

"What about Nadine?" Quinn asked. "She a meatball, too?"

"Oh, she couldn't kill her husband." Marci tried to mimic Nadine's voice. "Brandon was the kindest, most trusting person she knew."

Quinn laughed at the terrible impression. "A woman's got her needs."

"A woman's got her needs," Marci muttered. She turned to her computer and slapped the keyboard. "Tell me about it."

Quinn stared at his blank computer screen.

"What are you doing?" Marci asked.

"Thinking about what you said."

"About my needs? You need help, Quinn"

He faked a shiver. "God, no." He stood. "I'm going to head over to CTF and see if they can shine some additional light on the bikers."

Marci frowned. "Why not go over to SIU? They're the gang unit."

Quinn shrugged. "Morgan knows the bikers better than anyone."

Now, it was Marci's turn to shiver. "Ugh. Have fun with that."

***

The Criminal Task Force sat in the neighboring Monroe Court Building. The unit was created during the crack epidemic of the nineties before Quinn started with the department. Since then, the CTF had lost any traditional sense of mission. The Spokane Police Department kept it around with budget trickery and used it as a hammer to deal with problems not easily handled by patrol or other specialty units.

Most officers glorified the team, but Quinn disliked it. He thought it rife with cowboy mentality. Unfortunately, it seemed the current chief of police found the CTF more than helpful at times. Due to the team's longevity within the department, it was likely his predecessors had considered the unit useful as well.

Quinn entered the team's office. All the desks were staffed, which surprised him. He'd been in the office before and never found it fully operational. Someone was always in the field. The CTF was comprised of a sergeant, two detectives, and three officers.

Detective James Morgan looked up as Quinn approached. He put down his pen and squinted. The man was an enigma—a brute with a brain. Revered by many, hated by few. He'd survived multiple use of force and ethics complaints. Rumors circulated within the department about Morgan hobnobbing with judges, city council members, and defense attorneys.

Quinn sat uninvited in the chair across from Morgan. "Got a minute?"

"For you, Delaney," Morgan said, "I got two."

"I'll only need one," Quinn said. "What can you tell me about Wyatt Schulte?"

"Right to business, as always. What's your interest?"

"Homicide," Quinn said. "The one from Hamilton Street. His bike was on the flatbed. The victim, a guy named Brandon Rice, illegally towed it."

"Brandon Rice. Never heard of him." Morgan glanced around the office. The rest of the team eavesdropped on their conversation. All shook their heads at his silent question. "Why'd he pick up the bike?"

"Payback" Quinn said. "Wyatt was hooking up with his wife."

Morgan grinned. "Wyatt is a notorious poon hound. Guy gets out of jail and goes crazy for it. There's something about him that brings the women running. I would have figured the husband to do something stupid like challenge Schulte to a fight, not be suicidal and poach the man's ride."

Quinn leaned in, interested. "Do you think Wyatt would murder someone for stealing his motorcycle?"

"A Soul's bike is sacred territory. I could imagine just about anything happening." Morgan's head bounced from side to side. "Especially if it meant he had to drive a grocery-getter around for any length of time."

"You know what he drives?" Quinn asked.

Morgan grunted. "It's in the file. Most of them have a car for schlepping milk and eggs except it's usually the old ladies who drive them. With that said, there's no way I see Wyatt zapping someone on that corner at any time of day. It's too public. If he were going to do it, it would be done quietly where none of us would ever hear about it."

That was in line with Quinn's own thoughts. "How'd he earn the Widowmaker moniker?"

"It's an old eighties song," Morgan said. "One of those hair metal bands. He told me one time when we were making nice. I made a note about it in his file. We can look that up, too, if you think it's important."

Quinn waved a hand. "You think any of the Souls would have killed Rice that way?"

Morgan shook his head. "It's the same argument. The Souls are hot-tempered, but they're not stupid. That corner at that time of day—it's an audacious way to kill a man."

"Brazen," Quinn said, recalling Marci's words from earlier in the day.

"Detective Synonym," Morgan said. "I'll tell you this much. There's a fine line between bravery and stupidity. When the results are disastrous, it's easy to point to the latter. When the results resemble success is when it's hard to find the truth."

Quinn stood. "Thank you."

Morgan appeared perplexed. "I don't know what I did."

"You gave me some food for thought."

***

When Quinn arrived at his desk, he hung up his cell phone.

Marci looked over from where she sat. "You're back from The Land of Misfit toys."

"Let's go," he said. "Patrol found Raleigh Garmany." He turned and headed for the exit.

Marci hurried up to him. "What's with the look on your face?"

"Inspiration," Quinn said. "It's something Morgan said about bravery and stupidity."

She sniffed dismissively. "That guy should know."

"You said it was brazen for someone to kill Brandon

Rice at that corner this morning."

Marci nodded. "But maybe it was stupid."

"Or something in between." Quinn pushed open a door at the west exit.

He was lost in his thoughts.

***

A 7-Eleven stood at the corner of Second Avenue and Pine Street. Its vibrant colors, central location, and all-day operating hours were a beacon for the homeless population in the area. Clusters of dirty, shabbily dressed people milled about the property while citizens quickly pumped gas or hurried inside for a snack.

Three patrol cars parked in the lot and formed a triangle. Three officers and Raleigh Garmany stood in the middle.

Traffic backed up on Second as commuters rubbernecked. Several homeless men hovered nearby.

Raleigh seemed preternaturally calm as he leaned against the push-bar of one of the patrol cars. He wore a filthy white T-shirt, brown Carhartt pants, and leather sandals. His feet were dusty.

Patrol Officer Pauleen Sherman stepped away from the group. She was a tall, slightly overweight woman who carried a permanent look of pensive anger. She wore the black jumpsuit most of the department favored these days. "It's the professionals," she said.

Marci smiled. "Aw, you like us."

"Don't sprain your arm patting yourself on the back," Pauleen said. "I'm mocking your suits."

"Of course, you are." Marci smirked. "You're no fashion prize yourself."

Pauleen ran a hand along her side. "Any man would

be lucky to have a piece of this."

Marci snorted. "Any man would be lucky to survive a piece of you."

"You know it," Pauleen said.

From his position perched against the nearby patrol car, Raleigh Garmany scoffed. "You two wanna get a room?"

Pauleen turned. "Relax, buddy, they'll get to you soon enough."

"You got no right," Raleigh said. "I didn't do nothing."

Quinn moved closer. "Where were you this morning?"

Raleigh lifted his chin. "Who are you?"

"Detective Delaney." He motioned to Marci. "Detective Burkett."

"Never heard of you," Raleigh said.

"Answer their questions," Pauleen said. "We've all got better places to be."

Raleigh's face pinched. "You answer their questions. I didn't do nothing."

"Where's his stuff?" Quinn asked.

Pauleen pointed to a shopping cart loaded with items such as a soiled sleeping bag, grimy clothes, and worn-out shoes.

"Stay out of there," Raleigh said.

"Do you own a gun?" Quinn asked.

"A gun?" Raleigh searched the faces of the officers near him. "No." His eyes now locked onto Quinn's. "*No.*"

Marci's cell phone rang. She answered it and stepped away.

"Where were you this morning?" Quinn asked a second time.

Raleigh waggled a finger. "I wasn't nowhere if it had

something to do with a gun."

"You've been arrested with one in the past," Quinn reminded him.

"I learned my lesson." Raleigh glanced between the other officers. "I swear to God." He motioned to his shopping cart. "Check my stuff if you don't believe me."

The two patrolmen eyed Quinn. He lifted his chin toward the shopping cart full of grubby items. Both men grimaced. Quinn was sure they'd curse his name later.

Raleigh said, "Listen, Detective, I'm on a new path. I'm taking my meds and following the gospel."

One of the patrol officers lifted several pill bottles from the cart and shook them.

"See?" Raleigh said. "They've leveled me out. Quieted the voices." He tapped his temple. "I even got my ninety-day chip. She saw it." He lifted his chin in Pauleen's direction. "She confiscated it and put it in a plastic bag."

Pauleen motioned toward the hood of her patrol car. "There's a chip in there with the other stuff from his pockets. Doesn't guarantee he's clean."

"I am," Raleigh said. He faced Quinn. "I swear it."

"Why are you still out here?" Quinn asked.

"On the streets?" Raleigh spread his arms. "I like it. Listen, you don't have to be sick in the head to want to be free. That's something completely different than the drugs and the voices."

Marci covered her open ear with a hand. "Say that again," she said into the phone.

Quinn watched her for a moment before returning his attention to Raleigh. "When is the last time you spoke with your brother-in-law?"

"Brandon?" Raleigh shrugged. "Hell, I don't know. Not since last year, right before Thanksgiving, I think."

"Is that when he kicked you out of his house?" Quinn asked.

Raleigh's brow furrowed. "What are you talking about? Brandon never kicked me out."

Quinn nodded, playing along. "But you guys have fought, right? Our guys were even called to deal with you in the past."

"That was because of my sister winding me up," Raleigh said. "She did that so I would fight with Brandon and then she kicked me out because of it. She's crazy." He interlaced his fingers. "You gotta believe me, Detective. I'm totally neutral now. Wait. Did something happen to Brandon?"

"Something did happen, Raleigh," Quinn said. "Someone climbed up to the window of his tow truck and shot his brains across the cab."

"It wasn't me," Raleigh said. "Poor Brandon. That ain't right."

Marci ended her call. "Patrol found a business with some video of the incident."

Quinn watched Raleigh for his reaction, but the man seemed more concerned about learning about his brother-in-law's status.

"According to Silva, a green Jeep Wagoneer pulled into the lot," Marci said, then grinned.

Quinn was about to ask a question, but she cut him off.

"Wait. It gets better."

***

Nadine Rice opened the door to her home. She still wore the same flannel shirt as earlier, but she had changed her T-shirt to one featuring a Mötley Crüe logo.

Black Converse tennis shoes were now on her feet. "You're back."

Quinn asked, "May we come in?"

She eyed Marci. "Decided to try my tuna casserole, huh?"

"No," Marci said, "we have some follow-up questions."

Nadine stayed in the doorway. "I told you I don't know where my brother is."

"That's all right," Quinn said. "We found him."

She smirked. "That was fast. Still batshit crazy, huh?"

Quinn shook his head. "Actually, he's fine. He's on antipsychotics, attending counseling, and staying clean with the Lord's help."

She crossed her arms. "I'll believe that when I see it."

"Throws a wrench into your story," Marci said.

Nadine pursed her lips. "I don't know what you're talking about."

"How about this?" Marci said. "You called Brandon and asked him to meet."

"I told you it was about dinner," Nadine snapped. "You think I killed my husband?"

Marci ignored the question, continuing her story. "Shortly after that, a green Jeep Wagoneer pulled into the vacant lot at Mission and Hamilton."

"Oh, my God." Nadine's lip quivered. "Wyatt has a green Jeep."

"He does, but he wasn't driving," Marci said.

"It was somebody else's Jeep, then," Nadine said quickly.

"No, it was his." Marci shook her head. "You see, the dry cleaner across the street has video cameras. Seems they've suffered some break-ins. They caught you driving Wyatt's Jeep, walking up to the tow truck, then leaving."

Nadine smirked. "So what? I saw my husband. That doesn't prove anything. I didn't tell you because I didn't want it to get back to Wyatt and have him get jealous."

"Didn't you say Brandon was a figment of Wyatt's imagination?" Marci asked. "That it was like a wolf worrying about a house cat?"

Nadine shrugged off her words. "None of this proves anything."

"Maybe, maybe not," Quinn said. "We touched base with Wyatt before coming here and asked if you were driving his car today."

Nadine ran her tongue underneath her upper lip. "I don't believe you. He wouldn't say nothing that put me in jeopardy. That's not how he is."

Marci smiled. "I think you have a false impression of your boyfriend. Once we told him we had video of his car at the murder scene and you getting out of it, he told us how you drove him to the clubhouse and took the car shopping. When you brought it back, he took you home."

Nadine flicked her hand. "Whatever."

"Nadine Rice," Quinn said, "you're under arrest for the murder of your husband, Brandon Rice."

Her eyes darkened. "Good luck finding the gun."

"We won't need it," Quinn said. He grabbed her hand and pulled her out of the house. Marci took the woman's other wrist and slapped a handcuff on it. "You have the right to an attorney."

The detectives led Nadine down the steps to a waiting patrol car.

"You got it all wrong," Nadine said. Her voice was now soft and filled with uneasiness. "Brandon wasn't that good of a husband."

Marci lifted an eyebrow. "You said he was the kindest, most trusting man you knew."

Nadine twisted to look at Marci. "I was lying to not speak ill of the dead. You know how it is. But he beat me something fierce."

Quinn suspected Nadine's story had changed now due to her being caught. She wasn't the first person to do that once in custody and she certainly wouldn't be the last.

Nadine looked up at Quinn. Her face softened and her eyes misted. "I'm a battered woman."

"At the eleventh hour," Marci said.

Nadine squinted. It seemed as if she were trying to will tears to fall. "It's true. I had to stand up for myself. Brandon was going to hurt me because of Wyatt."

"Are you admitting you killed your husband?" Quinn asked.

Nadine's eyes shifted to Marci then back to him. The tenderness in her eyes dissipated, and she spat on the sidewalk. "I wanna talk to an attorney."

"When you get to jail," Quinn said. He protected Nadine's head as he guided her into the back of the patrol car. When she put her feet inside, he shut the door.

Notes

I miss buying music on cassettes. I also miss buying it on CDs or on vinyl. Part of the experience was reading the liner notes. I felt disappointed, almost cheated, if a band didn't include their lyrics. The streaming services have realized listeners appreciate them and include an option to view them now.

A song's words matter to me, especially if a singer mumbles, or the band overplays their front man. The lyric sheet helps a fan avoid embarrassing moments like Troy Pembrook's mangling of a Bon Jovi tune in my short story, "In the Pocket."

In that same vein, I've enjoyed the Notes section of short story collections. They give me an insight into a tale's journey or what authors might have been thinking when they wrote the pieces. I hope you find some value in this section as well.

Originally, I planned to write a short story collection based around the Hope Apartments. It would have been very much like the anthology, but all the stories would have been by me.

The idea to switch the project to a themed anthology sprouted, and it seemed like more fun. I had already written several stories set at or around the Hope. I took those tales and spread them through my first two collections, *Murder by Any Other Name* and *Black and Blue in the Lilac City*. *The Eviction of Hope* was to be a standalone project, and I had no intention of doing a follow-up anthology.

"Hope Evicted" finished the anthology, and it

allowed me to access some of my property management experience. Actually, the entire premise did as well.

Two characters—Joe and Tom—appeared courtesy of Joe Clifford and Tom Pitts. They contributed a story to the anthology, "Dead Beats Calling." I enjoyed their characters so much I asked for permission to have them appear in my short story. They agreed, and the two live on in infamy.

"Officer Safety" appeared in Code 4 Press's The *Tattered Blue Line: Short Stories of Contemporary Policing*. Outside of James Morgan, my cops in the 509 Crime Stories' version of the Spokane Police Department are upstanding citizens. However, that doesn't mean they don't make mistakes. That's what happened in "Officer Safety." The story's protagonists react poorly to a criminal's provocations. It's a human moment. Only comic book heroes can always shine as beacons of lights. Sometimes our heroes cannot meet the standards we hold for them.

That's what happened in this story, and the officers choose to solve the issue with creative report writing. Whether it's right or wrong is up to the reader to decide.

"Prologue for Disorder" and **"The Legend of Roy Utt"** appeared in *A Bag of Dick's*, the second 509 Crime Anthology.

I thought the title for this collection was brilliant since it was a reference to a Spokane icon, Dick's Hamburgers. At one crime convention, the book's name earned me a shout out from a well-known author as "the Bag of Dick's guy!" That was good for a few days' worth of laughs.

Despite that, the title worked against me in several ways. First, an Amazon title search results in a vast amount of non-book related items. That's not good for any title's discoverability. When I narrow the search field to only Kindle items, the results include sex-related books. Again, not good. It's a crime fiction book, not gay porn or frustrated mommy romps.

Second, I think having "dick" in the title put many readers off. I should have considered that, had a snarky giggle about the proposed name, then put it aside. The premise was good for an anthology, but I should have selected a different title.

What I did differently in this anthology was include a prologue—a short story to set up the entire premise. "Prologue for Disorder" worked like a charm (if I'm allowed to pat myself on the back) and sent the entire collection on a tear. I wish I would have done something like that with *The Eviction of Hope*.

Roy Utt first appeared in *The Blind Trust*, the third book in the 509 Crime Stories. He ran from Detective James Morgan and was ultimately caught. Roy might have been a disposable character, the kind we often encounter in crime fiction novels, but everyone has an opportunity to be the hero of their own story in the 509. That's what I did with Roy.

Joe and Tom appeared again after additional approval of their original creators, Joe Clifford and Tom Pitts. The scene behind the 7-Eleven is one of my all-time favorites. Even after repeated readings, I still laugh about the Willy Wonka interaction and the eventual meltdown over Veruca Salt.

"In the Pocket" is a previously unreleased story. When I first wrote it, I set the tale in Seattle. However, it never felt right. I often returned to the piece, but I never liked what I had done with it. As I set to develop this collection, I pulled out the story. I wanted to include it, but the Seattle location wouldn't allow it to fit. Once I committed to set it in Spokane, everything flowed. I essentially rewrote the piece, keeping only the core idea. I'm happy with it now after all these years of it languishing on my hard drive.

"Prologue to Mayhem," "The Reunion of Back Road Bobby and Transmission Jack," and **"Epilogue for a Living Legend"** all appeared in *Back Road Bobby and His Friends*, the third and final 509 Crime Anthology.

When I started *The Eviction of Hope*, I never thought there would be a second collection. When I began *A Bag of Dick's*, I knew for certain there would be a third. At that point, I wanted a trilogy of 509 Crime Anthologies. It seemed like the right option.

I learned from the previous collection and included a prologue story to set the whole book in motion. What I did differently in the third was to include a third tale as an epilogue so I could wrap it all up. I believe it worked well.

Joe and Tom returned in "Epilogue for a Living Legend." The creators of those two allowed me to include them in the last anthology. I hadn't intended for them to be the glue that held my trilogy together, but it sort of worked out that way. I only wanted them to appear since Roy Utt and Morgan appeared in "Prologue to Mayhem."

Detective Jim Morgan appeared in another author's story in *The Eviction of Hope*. So the only characters to appear in all three anthologies were Morgan, Joe, and Tom, but the latter two only appeared in all of my stories from the collections. That's why I think the dead beats were the glue that holds the anthologies together. Obviously, it didn't start out that way.

The last story, **"Towed Away,"** appeared in the Mysteries to Die For anthology, *Move It or Lose It*.

Mysteries to Die For also produces a podcast version of each included story. Their version of the tales included a break to allow for a recap of clues to assist the reader/listener in determining who the suspect was. It's a neat concept but not conducive for a collection like this. I edited out the break and brought it back to its original concept.

***

After I became familiar with an album, I rarely referred to the liner notes again unless I wanted to remind myself of a forgotten lyric. Then I would search the other listed songs for forgotten phrases.

I hope you've found something interesting in these Notes that you may want to recall someday. Maybe you'll open this book in the future, flip to this section, and reread the background on "The Legend of Roy Utt." Maybe that will get you to peruse some other thoughts and you'll recall how much you enjoyed Bobby's frustration with his father. Maybe you'll decide you've got some time to join those two for another trip up to Tonasket.

That's the beauty of music and the magic of short stories. They can whisk us away on little notice.

I hope you enjoyed this journey.

Colin Conway
April 2024

Did You Enjoy the Book?

Thank you for reading *When the Wicked Rest* and visiting the 509! I hope you enjoyed meeting some of the recurring characters. This is a continuing series with other characters occasionally stepping into the lead role. There are two parallel series to the 509 Crime Stories—the Flip-Flop Detective and the John Cutler mysteries. I hope you'll check them out.

I'm always grateful when a reader takes time out of their day to comment on one of my novels. If you do write a review, please email me, and let me know.

I'd love to say thanks!

About the Author

Colin Conway is the creator of the 509 Crime Stories, a series of novels set in Eastern Washington with revolving lead characters. They are standalone tales and can be read in any order.

He also created the Cozy Up series which pushes the envelope of the cozy genre. Libby Klein, author of the Poppy McAllister series, says *Cozy Up to Death* is "Not your grandma's cozy."

Colin co-authored the Charlie-316 series. The first novel in the series, *Charlie-316*, is a political/crime thriller described as "riveting and compulsively readable," "the real deal," and "the ultimate ride-along."

He served in the U.S. Army and later was an officer of the Spokane Police Department. He has owned a laundromat, invested in a bar, and run a karate school. Besides writing crime fiction, he is a commercial real estate broker.

Colin lives with his beautiful girlfriend, three wonderful children, and a codependent Vizsla that rules their world.

Find out more at colinconway.com.